Kansas City Star

Kansas City Star

By
Matthew Gene

Names, characters, businesses, places, events, and incidents are either the products of the author's imagination or used in a fictitious manner. Any resemblance to actual persons, living or dead, or actual events, is purely coincidental.

No part of this publication may be reproduced, stored in a retrieval system, or transmitted in any form or by any means, electronic, mechanical, photocopying, recording, or otherwise, without the written permission of the publisher.

Text Copyright © 2024 Matthew Gene

All rights reserved.
Published 2024
by Progressive Rising Phoenix Press, LLC
www.progressiverisingphoenix.com

ISBN: 978-1-958640-70-8

Printed in the U.S.A.
1st Printing

Cover image by Matthew Gene, Copyright: 2024, Used with Permission.

Title Page and Chapter Illustration by Matthew Gene, Copyright: 2024, Used with Permission.

Book and Cover design by William Speir
Visit: http://www.williamspeir.com

I'm the number one attraction every supermarket parkin' lot
I'm the king of Kansas City...

Kansas City star, that's what I are

- Roger Miller

To Karen:

To my constant, my life, and my love. It is indescribable the thanks you deserve. I have been lost for a while, being away from writing far too long. Your kind words, praise, and own devotion in your recent publication has inspired me beyond words.

- I love you,
M

CHAPTER 1

Jake "Tex" Walker was the kind of man people trusted without question. His smile, wide and genuine beneath the brim of his well-worn cowboy hat, could light up the dreariest of days. The children loved him, their parents adored him, and the whole town of Evergreen held him in the highest regard. Tex wasn't just a local celebrity; he was a pillar of the community.

Every weekday afternoon, after the kids were out of school, families gathered around their television sets to watch The Tex Walker Show. It wasn't the fanciest production—just Tex, a few hand-sewn puppets, and a painted backdrop of the Wild West—but it was more than enough. Tex taught kids how to tie knots, respect nature, and understand the value of honesty and hard work, all while brandishing his toy pistols and tipping his hat with a "Howdy, partner!" that could melt the coldest of hearts.

It wasn't just a show. It was a ritual, one that brought families together and connected the old with the young. In Evergreen, you didn't just grow up; you grew up with Tex. But outside the bright lights of the studio and the adoring eyes of the town, Tex, or Jake Walker, was just a man. And like all men, he had his vices.

* * *

The moon hung low in the sky that night, casting a pale glow over the expanse of Walker's ranch. The town of Evergreen lay miles behind him, and here, under the vast, star-speckled sky, Jake felt the weight of his solitude. It was nights like these that he indulged in the bottle, the warmth of the whiskey taking the edge off the quiet that pressed in around him.

He sat on the porch, his boots propped up on the railing, nursing a glass of something far stronger than the sweet tea he sipped on the show. The land stretched out before him, a dark ocean of rolling fields and dense woods. He often told people he loved the quiet, but the truth was, sometimes it was too quiet, too lonely.

Jake took another swig, the burn of the alcohol a familiar comfort. His thoughts drifted to the past, to the years before The Tex Walker Show, before he'd found his place in Evergreen. Back then, he'd been just another drifter, bouncing from town to town, trying to outrun his own failures. But the town had taken him in, and he'd built something good here, something he could be proud of.

A flash of light streaked across the sky, snapping Jake from his thoughts. He squinted, watching as it became brighter, closer. He tensed all over as it flared, crashing somewhere in the woods beyond his property with a distant, muffled thud.

"Damn," he muttered under his breath, standing and stumbling slightly as he found his balance. Maybe it was just a meteorite, or maybe some old piece of space junk that had finally lost its battle with gravity. Either way, it had landed close, too close to ignore.

His curiosity piqued, Jake grabbed a flashlight from inside the house and set off across the field. The tall grass brushed against his jeans; the cool night air sobering him up with each step. As he approached the woods, a strange unease settled over him, the kind that slithers up your spine and sits heavy in your gut.

He shook it off, pressing forward. The beam of his flashlight cut through the darkness, illuminating the narrow path that wound through the trees. Branches creaked and leaves rustled in the breeze, but otherwise, the night was still.

The smell hit him first, a sharp, bitter scent that stung

his nostrils. It wasn't the smell of burning wood or earth, but something else, something metallic and wrong. He quickened his pace, the tension growing with each step.

Finally, he reached a small clearing, and there, in the center, lay the object. It was partially buried in the ground, still glowing faintly. Jake approached cautiously, his flashlight dancing over its surface. It was smooth, almost reflective, and unlike anything he'd ever seen. It was too perfect, too precise to be a natural formation.

"What in the hell…" he murmured, reaching out to touch it.

The surface was cold, impossibly so, and as his fingers brushed against it, the object hummed, a low vibration that Jake could feel in his bones. He jerked his hand back, heart beating frantically. He stood there for a long moment, staring at the thing, trying to make sense of what he was seeing. It didn't belong here, that much was certain. *But what was it? And why had it fallen from the sky?*

Jake's first instinct was to call someone, maybe the sheriff, or even the nearest university. But, something held him back. This was his land after all. If this thing had fallen here, then didn't that make it his? Besides, who was to say what kind of trouble he'd bring down on himself by letting others know? Scientists, government men, they'd swarm his property like flies on a carcass, picking it apart and leaving him with nothing. No, this was something he needed to figure out on his own.

He took a deep breath, the cold air filling his lungs. He circled the strange thing in the field, trying to find any sign of damage, any clue as to what it was or where it had come from. But the more he looked, the less he understood. Finally, he made a decision. He couldn't leave it out here, not where someone else might stumble across it. With some effort, he managed to hoist the object from the ground and carry it back to the house. It was heavier than it looked, but not impossibly so, and despite its coldness, it didn't seem to harm him.

By the time he reached the porch, Jake was out of breath and sweating despite the chill. He set the thing down in one corner of the room and stared at it for a long time, the whiskey buzz long gone. He had no idea what he was dealing with, but his gut feeling was that this was the beginning of something, something big, and something dangerous.

Jake Walker had always been a man who believed in his own luck. But as he stared at the strange object, its surface catching the dim light of the room, he wondered if his luck had finally run out. And, somewhere deep inside him, a quiet voice whispered that maybe, just maybe, he should have left well enough alone.

Chapter 2

Jake couldn't sleep that night. He tossed and turned in his bed; the soft creak of the old mattress was the only sound in the room. His mind kept returning to the thing he'd found, now tucked away in the corner of his living room, wrapped in a heavy blanket to keep it out of sight. But out of sight didn't mean out of mind. Every time he closed his eyes, he saw it again: the strange, cold metal, and the eerie hum. He wasn't a superstitious man, but something about that thing unsettled him. It felt... alive, somehow. And that thought alone was enough to keep his eyes wide open, staring into the darkness.

Around three in the morning, Jake gave up on sleep. He climbed out of bed, threw on a pair of jeans and a flannel shirt, and made his way downstairs. The house was quiet, the kind of quiet that only comes in the dead of night, when the world feels like it's holding its breath. He paused at the bottom of the stairs, listening, half-expecting to hear something, anything that would explain the feeling gnawing at his insides, but there was nothing, just the steady ticking of the clock on the wall and the low drone of the refrigerator.

Jake turned on a lamp, the soft glow casting long shadows across the room. His attention drifted to the corner where he'd hidden the object. It was still there, of course, undisturbed, but something about it felt different. He couldn't put his finger on it, but the air in the room felt charged, as if it were radiating some kind of energy.

He approached it while his heart thumped hard in his chest. The blanket wrapped around it seemed to pulse, as if the thing beneath were breathing. Jake hesitated, then reached out, pulling the blanket away. The object looked the same as before—smooth, and utterly alien. But as he stared at it, he realized that something *had* changed. The surface, once flawless and cold, now had a faint crack running through it, a thin line that seemed to emit light from within.

He leaned in closer, trying to get a better look. As he did, the crack widened slightly, the glow intensifying. And then, without warning, it emitted a low, pulsating sound, louder this time, almost like *it* had a heartbeat. Jake jerked back, nearly stumbling over the coffee table in his haste to put some distance between himself and the object. The noise continued, becoming louder, filling the room with its strange, unsettling rhythm.

"What?..." he whispered, his voice barely audible over the noise.

Jake grabbed the blanket and threw it over the object again, trying to muffle the sound, but it was no use. The mysterious buzzing noise continued, vibrating through the floor, up through his legs, and into his chest. It felt like it was inside him, in sync with his own body.

Panic surged through him. He needed to get rid of this thing, and fast. But before he could move, the humming sound stopped as abruptly as it had started. The silence that followed was deafening, pressing in on him from all sides. He stood there, frozen, every muscle in his body tensed and ready to bolt, but nothing happened. It was silent, still, as if nothing had ever been wrong. He waited a few more minutes, his breath coming in short, shallow bursts, before finally letting out a shaky sigh. Maybe he was just tired, his imagination running wild in the middle of the night, maybe.

A soft, almost imperceptible click echoed through the room, cutting off his thoughts. He turned slowly, dread pooling in his gut. The sound had come from behind him, from the hallway mirror. Jake's reflection stared back at him, but there was something wrong. He stepped closer, squinting in the dim light. His reflection didn't move. Jake blinked, trying to clear the fog of sleep deprivation from his mind. He raised his hand and watched as his duplicate did the same, almost.

There was a slight lag, just a fraction of a second, but enough to set every nerve in Jake's body on edge. He moved it from side to side, watching as the other Jake followed, just about a half second behind.

"Weird..." Jake muttered, reaching out to touch the mirror.

His fingers met cold glass, but the reflection didn't mimic the movement. Instead, it stood there, hand raised, staring back at him with eyes that were no longer his own. Jake recoiled back into the living room. The mirror image stayed in the hallway, hand still raised, face twisted into a cruel mockery of his own.

"Who are you?" he whispered, voice trembling.

The image smiled, a slow, sinister grin that sent a shiver down Jake's spine. It was a smile that didn't belong on his face, a smile filled with malice and something else, something darker.

"I'm you," it said, though Jake never opened his mouth. The voice was his, but distorted, like it was coming from a great distance, warped and twisted by the miles.

"No," Jake shook his head, backing away. "No,

you're not."

"You brought me here," it said, taking a step forward, closer to the glass. "Now I'm free."

Jake's back hit the wall; this couldn't be real. It had to be a nightmare, some whiskey-fueled hallucination brought on by stress and lack of sleep. But the cold, creeping terror in his veins told him otherwise.

It reached out, placing its hand against the glass. The surface rippled, like water disturbed by a pebble, and for a moment, Jake thought he saw it pass through the glass entirely, fingers stretching into his reality.

"You can't run," the image whispered. "You can't hide."

Jake squeezed his eyes shut, willing the nightmare to end. This wasn't happening. This wasn't real. But when he opened them again, the other Jake was gone. The mirror was just a mirror, reflecting the empty hallway and the soft light of the living room.

He exhaled. His knees threatening to buckle below him. He didn't understand what was happening, but he knew one thing for certain, that strange thing in the living room was the cause of it all. He needed to get rid of it, and fast, before things got any worse. But even as the thought crossed his mind, a quiet, insidious voice whispered in the back of his head, telling him that it was already too late.

The next morning, Jake awoke with the first light of

dawn, his body aching from the fitful sleep he'd finally succumbed to. His mind was foggy, the events of the previous night playing over and over in his head, like a bad dream.

He dragged himself out of bed, every step feeling heavier than the last. As he reached the bottom of the stairs, he looked at the corner of the living room where the object lay, still wrapped in the blanket. It was silent now, as if nothing had happened. But Jake knew better.

He stood there for a long moment, staring at the shape, trying to decide what to do next. His first instinct was to take it as far away as possible, maybe bury it in the woods or throw it into the river. But something stopped him, an inexplicable pull that kept him rooted. As much as he wanted to be rid of it, Jake couldn't deny that a part of him was drawn to it. It was a dangerous curiosity, the kind that had gotten him into trouble more times than he cared to remember.

Finally, he tore his eyes away and went to the kitchen, deciding that a strong cup of coffee was what he needed to clear his head. But as he reached for the coffee pot, he froze. A wave of unease swept over him, an inexplicable sense that something was wrong. His eyes scanned the counter, but nothing was out of place. Still, the cold, creeping dread lingered, and he couldn't explain why. His heart raced, his mind running in circles, trying to make sense of the unsettling feeling. And then, as if on cue, the soft hum started up again, faint but unmistakable, coming from the living room.

Jake's mind raced. Something was happening, something he couldn't control or explain. And whatever it was, it wasn't over yet.

With a deep breath, he turned and walked back into the living room. The object was still under the blanket, but the noise continued, growing louder with each step. He didn't stop. He couldn't stop.

As he reached it, the sound crescendoed, flowing through his entire body. Jake pulled the blanket away once more. It still radiated light from the crack in its surface, now larger, pulsing with a strange, inner light. And then, the hum stopped, replaced by a single, deafening silence.

For a moment, he stood there, waiting for something, anything to happen. And then, slowly, almost imperceptibly, the surface of the object started splitting open. Jake watched, feeling his ears get hot from the blood rushing to his head.

Whatever was inside…he was about to find out.

Chapter 3

Jake's pulse quickened as he watched the object open. It was agonizing to watch, a slow speed, like the deliberate splitting of an ancient egg. The room grew colder, a deep, biting chill that seeped into him. The light emanating from it intensified, filling the room with an unnatural glow that cast eerie shadows on the walls. And then, with a soft hiss, the object's surface peeled back, revealing something inside.

Jake gasped as the inner chamber was exposed, revealing a small, intricately crafted mechanism. It was unlike anything he'd ever seen, a complex network of gears and wires, all connected to a central core that beat with a soft, rhythmic light. It was beautiful in a way, but there was something deeply unsettling about it as well. The mechanism hummed with life, the faint vibrations resonating through the floor. He leaned in closer, his curiosity battling with his fear. The mechanism seemed to draw him in, its strange, alien beauty captivating him, even as his mind shouted that something was terribly wrong. And then, without warning, the mechanism began to move. The gears clicked and whirred, the wires twitching like the tendrils of some mechanical creature. He stepped back, watching the device come to life.

The central core brightened, shifting from a soft blue to a deep, ominous red. The hum grew louder, a low, throbbing vibration that rattled the windows and sent a shiver down Jake's spine. And then, with a sudden burst, the mechanism expanded, unfolding like a metal flower. He shielded his eyes from the blinding light, his mind reeling as the object seemed to grow, its intricate parts spreading outwards, filling the room with its presence.

When the light finally dimmed, Jake lowered his hand, in shock at what he saw. The object had transformed, its once compact form now stretched and twisted into something unrecognizable. It was still made of the same smooth material, but now it resembled a strange, alien machine, one that defied explanation.

The central core surged with energy, the deep red casting out an unsettling light. Jake could feel the power flowing from it, a raw, pulsing force that seemed to course through the air. He stood back, his mind trying to make sense of what he was seeing. This *thing* was no ordinary piece of debris that had fallen from the sky. This was something else, something powerful, something dangerous. And it was awake.

Jake's first instinct was to run and to get as far away from this thing as possible. But before he could move, it emitted a soft, almost musical chime. The sound was beautiful, hauntingly so, and for a moment, he found himself frozen in place, his fear forgotten. The chime became louder, the notes resonating in his chest, filling him with a strange, almost hypnotic calm. The red light of the central core softened, shifting to a soothing blue, and he felt a wave of warmth wash over him. It was then that he realized it was communicating with him. The thought gave him goosebumps, breaking the spell that had held him captive. He shook his head, trying to clear his mind, but the chime continued, the notes weaving through his thoughts, pulling him back in.

Images began to flash before his eyes, strange, fragmented visions that made no sense. He saw a world bathed in light, its skies filled with towering structures of metal and glass. He saw creatures, unlike anything he'd ever imagined, moving through a city, their forms sleek and graceful, their eyes glowing with the same blue radiance that pulsed from the strange device. And then, he saw darkness, an endless void, swallowing and devouring the world. The creatures were gone, their city reduced to ruins, the sky filled with fire and ash. The chime grew louder, more frantic as the darkness closed in, threatening to consume everything.

Jake took a deep breath and braced himself. The images vanished as quickly as they had appeared, leaving him alone with the device. It was more than just a machine, it was a beacon, a message from another world, a warning of some great disaster. But why had it come to him? And what did it want?

The central core thumped again with the rhythmic blue light shifting to a deep, unsettling green. The device emitted a low, rumbling sound, a deep, guttural noise that seemed to vibrate through everything. He could feel the energy in the air growing thick with tension. It was changing again, its form twisting and warping, the once beautiful mechanism now a mass of jagged metal and sharp edges.

He backed away. Whatever this thing was, it was no longer friendly. The warmth he had felt moments ago was gone, replaced by a cold, calculating presence that filled him with dread. He needed to get out…now.

But as he turned to flee, it emitted a piercing screech, the sound so loud and jarring that it felt like a knife being driven into his skull. Jake cried out, clutching his head as the noise filled the room. And then, as suddenly as it had started, the screech stopped, leaving behind a heavy, oppressive silence.

He stumbled forward, his vision blurred, his ears ringing from the noise. He blinked, trying to clear his head, but everything was spinning, the walls warping and twisting in ways that made no sense. He could feel something pulling at him, a force dragging him back toward the device. He fought against it, but his legs felt like lead, his body heavy and unresponsive. And then, through the haze, he saw it, a figure, standing in the center of the room, right where the device had been.

It was tall, impossibly tall, its form sleek and alien. Its skin shimmered with the same metallic sheen as the device, its eyes illuminated with a deep, pulsating light. It had no face, no features, but Jake could feel its gaze on him, piercing through him, into his very soul.

The figure took a step forward, its movements smooth and fluid, like a predator stalking its prey. Jake tried to move, to run, but his body refused to follow through. He was frozen, trapped, as the creature closed in on him. Then, in a voice that was not a voice, that seemed to resonate from within his own mind, it spoke.

"I am free."

The words echoed through Jake's thoughts, filling him with a cold, paralyzing terror. He could feel the presence of the figure growing, expanding, filling the space around it with its dark, oppressive energy. It reached out, its hand stretching toward him, fingers long and sharp, like blades of metal. Then, with a touch that was both cold and searingly hot, it placed its hand on Jake's chest.

He screamed, the sound tearing through the stillness of the morning. Pain exploded through him, burning, as if his very soul was being ripped from his body. As the darkness closed in around him, Jake felt his mind shatter, his thoughts scattering like leaves in a storm. The last thing he heard before the darkness consumed him was the figure's voice, a whisper in the depths of his mind.

"You are mine."

When the sun climbed higher in the sky, casting its warm rays over Evergreen, no one noticed the absence of Jake Walker. The town was quiet, peaceful, and the streets empty in the early morning sun. The only sign that anything was amiss was the faint, rhythmic hum that echoed from Jake's house, a sound that went unnoticed by the waking world. And inside the house, standing in the center of the living room, was Jake, or at least something that looked like him.

It was perfect, an exact replica, down to the smallest detail. But there was something off about it, something in the eyes, the way they glowed with a faint, unnatural light.

It smiled, a slow, deliberate smile that didn't reach its eyes. It looked around, taking in its surroundings, its new home. With a quiet, satisfied hum, it stepped forward, ready to begin its new life.

Jake Walker was gone. But in his place, something new had been born. Something dark. Something evil. And it was hungry.

Chapter 4

When Jake, or the thing that had once been Jake, arrived at the studio the next morning, there was no hint of the horror that had unfolded the night before. The town of Evergreen was bustling with its usual morning activity, none the wiser to the dark force that now walked among them.

The studio was a small, unassuming building on the outskirts of town, its exterior weathered by years of harsh winters and humid summers. But inside, it was a place of joy, where The Tex Walker Show had been bringing smiles to the faces of children for nearly a decade. The crew greeted him with the usual smiles and nods, oblivious to the subtle change in him. Why would they notice? He was as much a fixture of Evergreen as the old oak tree in the town square. No one ever imagined that anything could be wrong with him.

As the new Jake walked through the studio, he moved with an unsettling ease, his stride a perfect imitation of the real Jake's relaxed, confident gait. He smiled at the makeup artist, waved to the cameraman, and even cracked a joke with one of the producers, everything just as it should be. Yet, for those who were paying attention, there was an undercurrent of something wrong, something elusive that lurked just beneath the surface of his affable demeanor.

The morning's filming went off without a hitch. The set was a cozy, colorful rendition of an old Western town, with wooden storefronts painted in bright hues, a saloon, and a dusty road that wound through the middle. The children's laughter echoed through the studio as they watched from behind the cameras, their faces filled with excitement as Tex Walker, their beloved cowboy hero, taught them about the importance of sharing and being kind to one another. But as the cameras rolled, something dark simmered in Jake's gaze, something that the children couldn't see, but the crew could sense it, even if they didn't understand it.

As the show went on, Jake's performance was flawless, too flawless, every line delivered with perfect timing, every gesture calculated to evoke just the right response. But there was an eerie precision to it, a coldness that hadn't been there before. Tex Walker, the warm and gentle cowboy, now felt more like a puppet, controlled by an unseen hand, performing a script that had been written long ago. The children, of course, didn't notice. They laughed and cheered as Tex tipped his hat and twirled his fake pistols, but the crew began to exchange uneasy glances. The producer, a middle-aged woman named Abigail, found herself frowning at the monitors, trying to pinpoint what was bothering her.

"Something's off," she murmured to herself, tapping a pen against her clipboard. "But what?"

Jake's eyes looked toward her for the briefest moment, the glow behind them darkening, but he quickly returned his attention to the cameras, the smile never faltering.

When the show wrapped for the day, the children were herded out by their parents, still buzzing with excitement. The crew began to pack up, their movements slower, more subdued than usual. The feeling that something wasn't right had settled over them like a thick fog, and they were eager to be done for the day. Jake remained on set, watching them with an intensity that made the hairs on the back of Abigail's neck stand up. She caught his eye and forced a smile, though it felt more like a grimace.

"Great show today, Jake," she said, her voice a little too loud. "The kids loved it, as always."

Matthew Gene

He smiled back, and briefly, Abigail thought she saw a flicker in his eyes, dark and predatory. "Thanks, Abi," he replied, his voice smooth and easy, just as it had always been. "Just doing my job."

She nodded. "Well, I'll see you tomorrow, then."

Jake nodded, but he didn't move. He just stood there, watching her with that same unsettling intensity. Abi turned away, hurrying to gather her things. She needed to get out of there; the longer she stayed, the more danger she was in. It was irrational, she told herself. This was Jake, their Jake. The man who had been the heart of this show for years. But the more she thought about it, the more she couldn't ignore that he had changed.

As she left, Abi glanced over her shoulder. Jake was still standing there, his silhouette dark against the bright lights of the set. He was watching her, and even from this distance, she could feel the weight of his stare.

She hurried to her car, the keys slipping from her trembling fingers as she tried to unlock the door. She finally managed to get inside, locking the doors. She started the car and pulled away, the feeling of Jake's gaze lingering, seeing her all the way home.

Jake lingered a while longer, his mind humming with the memory of the day's events. The show had gone well, but it was just the beginning. He could feel the power of the device coursing through him, filling him with a strength that the real Jake could never have imagined. He walked through the empty studio, his footsteps echoing off the walls. He could still hear the faint laughter of the children, their innocent joy resonating in his mind like a sweet, intoxicating melody. But there was more, an odd presence, dark and insatiable, lurking just under the surface. It whispered to him, urging him on, pushing him to do more, to take more. He smiled to himself, his eyes gleaming in the dim light. He would give the town what they wanted, what they expected. He would play his part perfectly, and no one would ever suspect a thing. But behind that perfect mask, the darkness would grow, slowly, steadily, until it could no longer be contained, and when that time came, Evergreen would know the true face of Jake Walker. For now, though, the new Jake had to prepare. There were things he needed to learn, people he needed to watch. He would be patient, bide his time, and when the moment was right, he would strike.

When he left the building and stepped out into the cool evening air, he glanced up at the sky, where the first stars were starting to twinkle in the fading light. The stars seemed different now, brighter, more vibrant, as if they were calling out to him, guiding him toward something greater. He liked it, welcomed it. Jake Walker's story was far from over.

Later that evening, as he sat in his living room, the air

still filled with energy. He stared at the object on the table, and felt a deep, resonant connection to it, as if it were a part of him. He could feel it pulsing, the energy flowing through him like a current, binding them together. The real Jake had been weak, limited by his humanity, by his fears and doubts. But now... now there were no limits.

He stood, and walked to the mirror in the hallway. He stared at his reflection, at the face that everyone knew and loved, and watched as the eyes shifted, glowing with an inner light. This was his life now, his world to shape as he saw fit, and he intended to do just that.

Jake turned and walked away. He had work to do, preparations to make, and soon, Evergreen would be his. The darkness within him stirred, eager and hungry, and it was only a matter of time before it would be unleashed.

Chapter 5

The days following the arrival of the new Jake were marked by a growing tension in Evergreen, though most couldn't quite put their finger on why. It was as if the town itself sensed the shift, a restlessness that settled within the people. But life in Evergreen continued as usual. The town was a place where everyone knew everyone, where secrets were hard to keep, and where the pace of life was slow and steady, untouched by the chaos of the larger world. It was the kind of town where people left their doors unlocked at night, where the biggest events were the annual fairs and the Friday night football games. Yet, beyond the surface of this idyllic community, something bad had started to stir.

Jake moved through the town like a shadow, blending in seamlessly with the people who loved and admired him.

He was the same man in appearance, same easy smile, warm voice, and familiar swagger, but those who looked closely could see the difference, though they didn't understand what it was.

Abi couldn't shake the feeling that something was wrong. The discomfort she had felt that first day hadn't lessened; if anything, it had grown stronger. She found herself watching him more closely, studying his movements, his expressions, trying to understand what had changed. It was subtle, she knew that much. He still performed his duties with the same enthusiasm, still charmed the children and parents alike. But there was a coldness to him now, a calculated precision to his actions that hadn't been there before. It was as if he was playing a role, and while he played it well, something was missing, something human. She wasn't the only one who noticed. Others in the crew had begun to talk, whispering in hushed tones when they thought he wasn't around. They spoke of the change, of how he seemed different, off somehow. But no one could say for sure what it was, and no one dared to confront him about it. For the children, however, Jake was still their beloved Tex Walker. They didn't see the darkness lurking behind his eyes or notice how his smile never quite seemed genuine. They still laughed at his jokes, still cheered when he twirled his fake pistols, still idolized him as their hero, but even among the children, there were whispers. A few of the older ones, the ones who had grown up watching Tex on their screens, began to feel wary around him. They couldn't explain it, couldn't put it into words, but they knew something wasn't right. And then, there were the dreams.

It started with one or two children who woke in the middle of the night, trembling and crying, unable to remember what had frightened them so badly. As the days passed, more and more children began to have the dreams, dark, twisted nightmares filled with shadows and whispers, where Jake Walker's face loomed large, his eyes radiating with that haunting glow. The parents dismissed it at first, chalking it up to overactive imaginations or too much TV before bed, but as the nightmares spread, so did the fear. Children who had once eagerly looked forward to seeing Tex Walker now hesitated, clinging to their parents' hands when they passed him on the street.

Jake noticed the change. He could feel the dread growing, spreading like a virus through the town, and he reveled in it. The evil inside him fed on it, becoming stronger with each passing day, but it wasn't enough. He had a plan, one that was slowly taking shape in his mind. He knew he had to be careful, to bide his time. The real Jake had been too beloved, too trusted. If he acted too quickly, the town would turn against him, and his plans would be ruined. So, he played his part, wearing the mask of the old Jake, blending in with the people of Evergreen, all the while carefully laying the groundwork for what was to come.

It started small, with little things that went unnoticed by most. A misplaced word here, a slip of the tongue there. He began to plant seeds of doubt, whispering rumors into the ears of those who would listen, sowing discord among the townspeople. And then, he began to push the boundaries of his role, testing the limits of what he could get away with. At first, it was subtle, a slight change in the tone of his voice when he spoke to the children, a lingering touch that made them squirm, but as the darkness inside grew, so did his boldness.

One evening, as the sun dipped below the horizon and the streets of Evergreen began to empty, Jake found himself at the local park. It was a quiet place, with swings and slides that creaked in the wind, and benches where the old folks sat to watch the world go by. But now, in the gathering dusk, the park was empty, save for one little girl.

She couldn't have been more than six or seven, with blonde pigtails and a pink dress that billowed in the breeze. She was alone, pushing herself on the swing, her small legs kicking out in front of her. Jake watched her from the shadows; he felt twisted feelings stir inside. He could smell her fear, taste it in the air, even though she didn't realize she was afraid.

He stepped out of the shadows, moving silently across the grass. She looked up as he approached, her face lighting up with a smile when she recognized him.

"Hi, Mr. Walker!" she called out, her voice bright and innocent.

He smiled. "Hello there, little lady," his voice smooth and warm, the perfect imitation of the real Jake. "What are you doing out here all by yourself?"

She shrugged, still swinging. "Mommy said I could play until it got dark."

"Well, it's getting dark now. Shouldn't you be heading home?"

She glanced around the empty park. "I guess so," she said softly.

He stepped closer, roiling with anticipation. He could feel the hunger rising, the need to feed on her fear. "Let me walk you home," his voice was low and soothing. "It's not safe for a little girl to be out here all alone."

Uncertainty crossed her face, but then she smiled and nodded, trusting him as all the children of Evergreen did. After all, he was Tex Walker, the cowboy who had always been there for them.

Jake held out his hand, and the girl took it without hesitation. His grip was firm, his skin cold against hers, but she didn't pull away. Together, they walked through the park, the shadows stretching longer as the last of the daylight faded away.

As they neared the edge of the park, he glanced down at her. For a moment, he imagined what it would be like to let the darkness out, to let it consume her, feeding the hunger inside him. But he held back, knowing it wasn't time yet. He had to be patient, had to wait for the right moment. For now, he would play his part, bide his time.

"Here we are," Jake said as they reached the edge of the park. He could see the girl's house in the distance, the porch light glowing like a beacon in the dark. "You run along home now."

The girl smiled up at him, "Thank you, Mr. Walker," she said, and with a quick wave, she turned and ran towards her house.

He watched her go, his smile fading as she disappeared into the distance. He simmered, hungry and impatient. Soon, he thought. Soon, they would all know the truth.

Jake had learned to mimic the real Jake perfectly, down to the smallest detail, and no one suspected a thing. He knew Abi was watching him, that she was suspicious. He could see it in her eyes, in the way she looked at him when she thought he wasn't paying attention. She was a threat, and threats needed to be dealt with. But not yet. He had a plan, one that would allow him to fully take control of Evergreen, to bend the town to his will. The incident at the studio had been a test, a small demonstration of the power he now wielded. With the darkness inside him growing stronger with each passing day, he was becoming more than just a mimic. He was evolving, changing, and soon, he would be unstoppable. But first, he needed to remove the obstacles in his path.

Abi was the biggest threat, but she wasn't the only one. There were others in the town who had begun to notice the change in him, who had started to whisper behind his back. They needed to be silenced before they could cause any real damage. Then there was the device, the alien technology that had given him life. It was still hidden in the house, dormant for now, but he could feel its power throbbing in the back of his mind, urging him to complete the transformation. He needed to activate it fully, to unlock its true potential. Doing so would require a sacrifice, one that would cement his control over the town and ensure that no one would be able to stop him. Jake's eyes glistened with a dark, poisonous light, his mind swirling with possibilities. The time was almost right. Soon, very soon, he would make his move, and when he did, Evergreen would never be the same.

The days turned into weeks, and the tension in Evergreen continued to grow. The nightmares continued, spreading from child to child like a plague. The whispers grew louder, the rumors more persistent. Something was wrong with Jake Walker, they said. Something had changed. But no one questioned him, not directly. Instead, they watched him from a distance, their smiles becoming more forced, their laughter more strained. And all the while, he watched them, waiting for the moment when his true self could be unleashed.

It came one late afternoon, during the taping of The Tex Walker Show. The children were gathered in the studio, their eyes filled with excitement as they waited for their beloved cowboy to take the stage. However, there was a tension in the air, a feeling of anticipation that made Abi nervous.

She had been watching Jake closely in the days leading up to this, her discomfort now more with each passing moment. There was something wrong, she was sure of it now. The man on that stage wasn't Jake Walker, at least not the one she had known for years, but she didn't know what to do. *How can I explain it to anyone else? How can I make them see what I see?* Most of the children still loved him and hung on his every word, but Abi could see how some of them hesitated now, shrinking back when he came too close.

As the cameras rolled, Jake stepped onto the set, his smile full and warm as ever. The children cheered, their faces lighting up with joy, but as he began his usual routine, Abi noticed something different about him, something cold and calculating.

He was playing his part perfectly, but there was a hunger that hadn't been there before. It was as if he was feeding off their joy, growing stronger with every laugh, every cheer. And then, without warning, his smile faltered and his eyes changed. For a brief moment, Abi saw something else there, something alien and terrifying. The children didn't notice, but she did. She froze, as she watched his expression change, his smile twisting into something cruel and animalistic.

The malice was rising, pushing against the boundaries of the mask he wore. He could feel it, like a storm building inside him, ready to burst forth and consume everything in its path. He held it back, barely. He had to be careful, had to wait for the right moment. He couldn't let it all go, not yet. But soon, soon they would all see. As the show continued, he felt the evil, more impatient. The children were oblivious, laughing and cheering as Tex Walker led them through another adventure. Abi couldn't ignore the feeling that something terrible was about to happen. And then, it did.

As the cameras rolled, and Jake delivered his lines with the usual charm, the lights in the studio began to flicker. It was subtle at first, just a brief dimming that no one seemed to notice. But then, the flickering grew more intense, the lights flashed on and off in rapid succession. The children's laughter faded, their excitement turning to confusion. Abi's heart raced as she watched Jake's face, something seeming to brew from within. The lights went out completely. The children gasped, their voices rising in panic as they called out for their parents, for Tex Walker, for anyone.

Abi stood still, watching Jake's silhouette in the dark. She could feel the tension in the air. Then, in the pitch blackness of the studio, she heard it, the low, rumbling growl of something that was not Jake. It was the sound of the hunger that had been building inside him finally breaking free.

The lights came back on, and for a moment, Abi saw him standing in the center of the stage, his face contorted into a sinister mask, his eyes alight with a malevolent glow. The children screamed, their fear palpable as they scrambled to get away, but Jake only smiled. He was now looking at Abi.

"Run," he whispered, his voice a low, menacing growl. The lights went out again. Abi didn't need to be told twice. She turned and ran from the studio while the children's screams echoed in her ears. But as she ran, she knew there was no escaping what was coming. Evil had been unleashed, and there was no turning back.

The following day, the town of Evergreen was in

shock. The news of what had happened at the studio spread like wildfire, the rumors more exaggerated with each retelling. Some said it had been a power outage, a simple technical malfunction that had caused the panic. Others whispered of something more sinister, something that couldn't be explained, but Abi knew the truth. She had seen it in Jake's eyes. Whatever had taken his place was not the man they had known and loved. It was something else, something dark and evil, and it was only a matter of time before it would strike again.

Most people couldn't pinpoint why they felt unsettled around him; they simply sensed a change they couldn't define. Conversations grew quieter in his presence, not yet fear, but something close—something that hovered on the edge of understanding.

Abi felt a sense of urgency growing inside her. She had seen too much to ignore the signs, and she knew she had to act soon, before whatever had taken hold of Jake fully revealed itself.

Chapter 6

Jake was feeling restless and agitated. As he rummaged through the cabinets, he came across a dusty bottle of whiskey shoved to the back of a shelf. He eyed it curiously, unsure at first what it was. But as he twisted the cap open and took a tentative sip, he felt the liquid burn down his throat. He was surprised by the warmth spreading through his body, a strange, unfamiliar sensation. Unsure whether he liked it, he drank some more, feeling his thoughts grow fuzzy, the edges of his anger blurring. Now, with the alcohol coursing through his veins, he felt a reckless surge of boldness, an urge to let go, to embrace the chaos inside.

He left the house, shadows closing in around him as he walked...

***

The sun was high in the sky, casting its relentless heat over the town of Evergreen. The streets were quiet, the usual hustle and bustle of the day subdued as the townsfolk went about their business. The events of the past few days had left the town on edge, and whispers of strange happenings had spread like wildfire. But on this particular day, the quiet was broken by the sound of unsteady footsteps and the unmistakable clink of a glass bottle against a belt buckle.

Jake stumbled down the sidewalk, his eyes bloodshot and unfocused. He wore his signature chaps from the Tex Walker Show over his faded blue jeans, but they were the only part of his usual attire that remained. Even the top button on his jeans and the buckle on his chaps were undone, flopping with every step he took. His shirt was missing, his bare chest streaked with dirt and sweat, and his face bore the marks of a recent fall—scratches and bruises that he didn't seem to notice or care about. In his hand, he clutched a nearly empty bottle of whiskey, the amber liquid sloshing around as he staggered toward the local Walmart. His steps were unsteady, his gait uneven as he swayed back and forth, barely able to keep himself upright.

The few people who saw him hurried to cross the street, their eyes wide with shock and disbelief. Jake Walker, the beloved children's TV show host, the man who had been a pillar of the community, was now a shadow of his former self—a drunk, disheveled figure who seemed to be falling apart before their very eyes.

As he stumbled down the street, his thoughts drifted as they often did these days, to Abi. Even through the haze of alcohol and darkness, she was there, a constant presence in his mind. He thought of the times they had worked together on local projects, the way she always seemed to know just what to say to make him laugh, or how her smile could brighten even his darkest days. Jake had never told her how he felt. He had always been too busy, too focused on his career, and worried about what people would think. But now, in his moments of clarity, he regretted that more than anything. He had let the chance slip away, and now it was too late.

He reached the Walmart parking lot and paused, swaying slightly as he looked around. The familiar sight of the large, colorful sign, the rows of cars, and the people going in and out of the store seemed to ground him for a moment. But then, his eyes landed on the row of mechanical rides near the entrance—the kind meant for children, with their bright colors and cheerful music. A slow, sloppy grin spread across Jake's face as he staggered toward one of the rides—a horse that played a tinny, carnival-style tune through speakers hidden in its sides. The horse was painted a garish red and gold, its mane a mass of stiff, plastic strands, and its saddle well-worn from years of use.

He chuckled to himself as he approached it, the sound low and rough in his throat. He swayed on his feet, his hand reaching out to steady himself against the horse's neck.

"Howdy there, partner," he slurred, his voice thick with alcohol. "Mind if I take you for a spin?"

With a grunt of effort, Jake hauled himself onto the ride, moving slowly and uncoordinated. He slumped onto the saddle, his legs dangling on either side, the bottle of whiskey still clutched in his hand. For a moment, he sat there, swaying slightly as he fumbled with his jeans pocket. After a few clumsy attempts, he managed to pull out a single quarter, the coin shimmered dully in the sunlight. His hands trembled as he tried to slide it into the slot on the side of the horse. The quarter slipped from his fingers once, clattering to the ground. But he quickly snatched it back up, muttering under his breath. On the second try, the coin finally dropped into place.

The ride began to groan and whir as its mechanism struggled under Jake's weight. After all, the ride was meant for children, and it struggled to lift and lower him as it slowly rocked back and forth. The music played on, a haunting, off-key melody that echoed through the parking lot.

As he leaned back in the saddle, his mind drifted

again, this time to the last conversation he had with Abi. She had been so concerned about him, her brow furrowed in that way she always did when she was worried. She had asked him if he was okay, and he had brushed her off, too proud to admit that something was wrong.

"Why didn't I just tell her?" He muttered to himself, barely more than a whisper. "Why didn't I just say…?"

But the words were lost, drowned out by the fog in his mind and the mournful tune of the mechanical horse. As people passed by on their way into the store, they gave Jake a wide berth, their expressions a mix of pity and fear. Parents hurried their children along, shielding them from the sight of the once-beloved TV star turned vagrant.

Jake noticed the looks, the way people were avoiding him, and it only fueled his anger. He took another swig of whiskey, the liquid spilling over the sides of the bottle as his hand trembled.

"Hey! Don't you walk away from me!" he shouted at a man who was pulling his young daughter toward the entrance of the store. He was loud and slurred, the words tumbling out in a jumbled mess. "I'm still Jake Walker! I'm still… I'm still Tex!"

The man didn't respond, didn't even look back as he quickened his pace, his daughter clinging to his side.

His face twisted, his grip tightening around the bottle. "Cowards," he muttered under his breath, his voice a low growl. "All of you... just a bunch of cowards."

He drooped further in the saddle, his head lolling back as the ride continued its slow, creaking movement. The bottle slipped from his grasp, clattering to the ground and spilling its contents onto the pavement. He didn't seem to notice, his eyes half-closed as he stared up at the sky, the sun blinding him with its harsh light. The world seemed to spin around him, the edges of his vision blurring as the alcohol took full effect. But even in his drunken stupor, the darkness inside him was still there, whispering in the back of his mind, feeding on his anger and despair.

"Tex Walker," Jake muttered. "Tex Walker's dead... and so are you."

The words hung in the air, heavy with the weight of truth. Jake Walker was gone—replaced by something darker, something twisted and broken.

As he sat there, collapsed on the horse, the tinny music playing on, two police officers approached him, their expressions stern. They had been called to the scene by concerned citizens who didn't know what else to do or how to handle their former local hero, now a public spectacle.

"Mr. Walker," one of the officers said gently, stepping forward. "Jake, it's time to go home."

Jake's eyes opened, bloodshot and unfocused as he looked at the officer. For a moment, there was a flash of recognition, a glimmer of the man he had once been. But then it was gone, replaced by a blank, hollow stare.

"Home?" he echoed, as if the word didn't quite register. "I don't... I don't have a home."

The officer exchanged a worried glance with his partner, then reached out his hand to help Jake down from the horse. "Come on, Jake. Let's get you out of here."

He didn't resist as the officer gently helped him down from the ride, his legs wobbling. The second officer moved in to steady him, and together they led him toward the waiting patrol car.

As they walked, Jake spoke incoherently under his breath, his words a jumbled mix of nonsense and bitterness. The officers shared uneasy glances, unsure of what to make of the man who had once been the pride of Evergreen but was now a broken shell.

They helped Jake into the back seat of the police car, the door closing with a heavy thud. The officers were both well aware that public intoxication was a chargeable offense. Under normal circumstances, they would have taken anyone else straight to jail. But this wasn't just anyone—this was Jake Walker. Despite the slurred words and his appearance, they could still see the man he used to be, and they both felt a deep sense of pity. He wasn't a criminal; he was someone who had lost his way, spiraling into a darkness they couldn't fully understand. They knew he needed help, not a cell, so they decided to take him home as a warning, hoping he'd find a way back to the man he once was.

"Let's get you home, Jake," one of the officers said gently, trying to offer some semblance of comfort. "Take it easy tonight, okay?"

Jake didn't respond, his head leaning back against the seat, his eyes unfocused as the car pulled away from the Walmart.

As the car left the parking lot, the townspeople who had witnessed the scene slowly began to disperse, the whispers growing louder as they shared what they had seen. Something had changed, something dark and terrible, and they could feel it, but no one knew just how deep that darkness went, or how far it would spread before it was done.

Chapter 7

The people of Evergreen went about their daily lives; the tension had now settled like a heavy fog. There was an unspoken agreement to avoid discussing the strange occurrences that had begun to permeate their lives.

Abi had become increasingly concerned. She knew that something terrible was brewing, something connected to Jake. The incident at the studio had only confirmed her worst fears. The children's panic, the flickering lights, and the strange, almost malevolent energy that had filled the room that day were all too real. Abi had tried to convince herself that it was just a technical glitch, a power surge that had rattled everyone's nerves, but deep down, she knew the truth. Jake was no longer Jake.

Abi spent sleepless nights pouring over the details,

trying to piece together what had happened. She revisited old recordings of the show, watching them closely, looking for any signs of the change. The more she watched, the more convinced she became that something had happened to Jake, something that had turned him into the creature that now wore his skin. She had to act, but she had to be careful. Jake remained a beloved figure in Evergreen, and any accusation against him would be met with disbelief and hostility by those still oblivious to his change. She needed proof, something concrete that she could show the authorities, something that would make them see what she saw. She couldn't focus on her work, couldn't eat, couldn't sleep. All she could think about was Jake and the darkness that had taken root in him. She had tried to reach out to others, to subtly gauge their feelings about him, but most seemed blissfully unaware of the danger. She was running out of time, and unsure how to stop it. She was just one person, and Jake was far more powerful than she could have ever imagined. Desperation drove her to act. She needed answers, needed to understand what had happened to him, and there was only one place she could go to find them: Jake's house. It was a risk, a dangerous one, but Abi knew she had no other choice. If she could find something, anything that would explain the change in Jake, she might be able to convince the authorities, or at the very least, protect herself from whatever he had become.

So, late that afternoon, Abi made her way to Jake's house. The streets were quiet, the air cool and still. She tried her best to stay hidden along the way as she approached the old, weathered house.

His house was on the outskirts of town, nestled in a small grove of trees. It was a modest place, unremarkable in every way, but as Abi drew closer, a strange sense of foreboding washed over her. The house seemed different now, darker, more menacing, as if it were a living thing waiting to devour her. Abi pushed the fear aside. She had come too far to turn back now.

Her phone buzzed with a new text message:

Abi, OMG! Did you hear about Jake? He's drunk at Walmart. I just heard. The police are there now. Not sure what's happening.

Abi knew then she had to act fast, praying he wouldn't return too soon. Maybe he'd go to jail, and that would buy her plenty of time.

The front door was unlocked, just as she had expected. She slipped inside, her breath catching in her throat as she stepped into the dimly lit hallway. The house was quiet, only the faint creak of the floorboards. She moved carefully, her eyes scanning the shadows for any sign of movement. She had to be quick; if Jake returned and found her here, she didn't know what he might do.

She walked through the house, searching for anything

that might give her answers. However, the house was strangely empty, devoid of any personal belongings or signs of life. It was as if Jake had stripped away all traces of the man he had once been, leaving nothing behind. Then, in the living room, Abi found it.

It was sitting on a small table in the corner of the room, partially covered by a blanket, but even from a distance, Abi could feel the power emanating from it—a cold, pulsing energy that made her skin crawl. She approached it slowly, her hands trembling as she reached out to pull the blanket away. The device was unlike anything she had ever seen—smooth, metallic, alien in design, and *egg-shaped*, she thought. It hummed softly, the sound vibrating through the entire house. She stared at it. This was the device that had started everything, the thing that had drawn out the darkness in Jake. But what could she do with it? How could she stop it?

Her thoughts were interrupted by the sound of the front door opening, followed by a heavy, uneven shuffle. Abi's heart pounded in her chest—someone was there. She crept toward the window, peeking out just in time to see a car pulling away. Her breath seized as she recognized the distinctive markings of a police cruiser. Panic surged through her. Jake was home. She could hear his unsteady footsteps entering the house, his breathing heavy and ragged, punctuated by mumbled curses. The alcohol was evident in the slur of his words and the clumsy sound of his steps. She had no time to think, no time to hide. She grabbed the blanket and threw it back over the device, then ducked behind the couch. She could hear his footsteps in the hallway, slow and deliberate. He was moving through the house, searching for something, or someone.

Abi tried to steady her breath, to remain calm. If he found her, she was certain he would kill her. She needed to get out, to escape before it was too late. But as Jake entered the living room, she realized with a sinking feeling that there *was* no way out. He was blocking the only exit, and the windows were too small to climb through. She was trapped.

Jake stopped in the center of the room, his eyes scanning the darkness. Abi held her breath, praying that he wouldn't see her, that he would just leave.

His gaze settled on the blanket-covered device, and a smile spread across his face. His voice broke the tense silence, slurred and low. "So... you've found it," he muttered, his grin crooked and unfocused. He took a step towards the couch, but his movements were slow and uncoordinated. The alcohol had dulled his senses, giving Abi a fleeting chance to escape. Her heart sank. He knew she was there. He had known all along.

Jake took another step, his eyes gleaming. "I've been expecting you, Abi," he said. "I knew you wouldn't be able to resist."

Abi could hardly breathe. She slowly rose from behind the couch, her eyes locked on Jake's. "What have you done, Jake?" she whispered, her voice trembling.

"I've become something more," he said, his voice filled with a twisted sense of pride. "I'm not Jake anymore. I'm something better."

She took a step back. She needed to get out of there, needed to find a way to escape. But Jake was between her and the door, and she knew he wouldn't let her leave.

"Why are you doing this?" Her heart pumping hard as she stared into the eyes of the man she had once trusted, someone she had worked with, laughed with, and called a friend. But, this wasn't that man anymore.

"Why are you doing this, Jake?" She asked again. She needed to understand, to know what had happened to him, even as she feared the answer.

Jake tilted his head, considering her question. "Why?" he repeated, his tone almost playful. "Because I can, Abi. Because the power that's been given to me is beyond anything you could comprehend. Jake Walker was just a man, a weak, insignificant man. But I am something more. I am evolution, the next step in what it means to be human."

Abi took another step back, her eyes darting toward the door, but Jake saw the movement and blocked her path with a single, deliberate step.

"You can't leave, Abi," he said softly, his voice carrying a chilling finality. "Not now. Not after you've seen."

Abi realized the full extent of the danger she was in. She was alone in the house, miles from help, with no way to escape this monster. Her mind searched for a way out, a way to survive. Then, her eyes fell on the device, still covered by the blanket, humming softly. If this device had played a part in Jake's transformation, perhaps it could be used against him.

"What is that thing?" Abi asked, gesturing toward the device, trying to buy herself some time.

Jake's eyes flashed with a dark amusement as he glanced at the device. "That, Abi, is the future. It's the key to everything, to power, to knowledge, to immortality. It's the reason I'm here."

She had to keep him talking, had to find a way to get to the device. "And what exactly are you?"

Jake's smile faded, replaced by a look of cold, calculated cruelty. "I am what humanity has always feared, I am the darkness that lurks in the shadows, the thing that wears a familiar face but is anything but human. I am the predator, and you, Abi, you're just the prey."

The words sent a shiver through her, but she forced herself to stay calm, to think clearly. She needed to distract him, needed to get closer to the device. "You don't have to do this," she said. "Jake, if there's any part of you left in there, you can stop this. You can fight it."

Jake's laughter was cold and cruel. "Jake is gone. There's nothing left of him but memories, and soon, even those will fade."

Abi took a deep breath, preparing herself for what she had to do. She had only one chance, and she had to make it count. With a sudden burst of adrenaline, she lunged for the device, ripping the blanket away and grabbing it with both hands. The cold metal vibrated against her skin, and for a moment, she felt as if the device was alive, pulsing with a strange, otherworldly energy.

Jake's expression shifted from amusement to fury as he realized what she was trying to do. "No!" he roared, running toward her with a speed and ferocity that was anything but human, but Abi was faster, this time. With a desperate cry, she pressed down on the central core of the device, her fingers fumbling for some kind of switch or button. The device hummed louder, its vibrations intensifying as it began to glow with a brilliant blue light.

Jake was almost on her, his eyes filled with rage. The light from the device flared, blindingly bright, and a wave of energy exploded outward, knocking Jake off his feet and sending him crashing into the wall. Abi was thrown back as well, the force of the blast sending her sprawling across the floor. The room shook, the walls vibrating with the intensity of the energy that had been unleashed.

For a moment, there was only silence, the air thick with the smell of ozone. Abi lay on the floor, gasping for breath, her body aching from the impact. Then, she heard it, a low, pained groan from across the room. She forced herself to sit up, her eyes searching the darkness for any sign of Jake. He was slumped against the wall, his body trembling, his eyes squeezed shut in pain, but something was different. The sinister light that had burned in his eyes was gone, replaced by something else, something that looked almost like fear.

Abi crawled toward him. She didn't know what the device had done, but it had clearly affected him. "Jake?"

He opened his eyes, and for a moment, she saw a glimpse of recognition, of something human, before it was replaced by a cold, hard glare. "You think you've won?" he hissed. "You think this changes anything?"

Abi felt a surge of anger, of defiance. "I don't know what you've become, but I know you can be stopped."

He laughed, a harsh, bitter sound. "You're a fool, Abi! You have no idea what you're dealing with. The device, it's just a tool, a means to an end. You can't stop me. No one can."

"Maybe I can't stop you, but I can try." she said.

Before Jake could react, Abi grabbed the device once more, her fingers searching for a way to activate it again, but this time, the device remained silent, its glow fading, the energy it had unleashed now spent.

Jake's laughter echoed through the room, with triumph. "You see? It's over, Abi. You've lost."

But Abi wasn't giving up. She wasn't sure what she was doing, or how she was going to do it, but she had to keep trying. And then, the device pulsed one last time, the glow flickering in its core.

Jake's laughter was replaced with confusion. "Wait! What are you doing?" he demanded, looking at the device.

Abi didn't know. She had to keep going, to keep fighting, even if she didn't fully understand what was happening. The device began to hum again, the light growing stronger, and Jake's expression shifted to terror.

"No!" he screamed, scrambling to his feet, his hands reaching out to stop her, but it was too late. The light from the device flared once more, brighter and more intense than before, and Abi felt a surge of energy pulse through her, filling her with a strength she didn't know she possessed. Jake was thrown back again, crashing into the wall with a sickening thud. This time, he didn't get up. The light faded, the device falling silent once more, and Abi collapsed to the floor.

She realized she had barely made it out of Jake's house with her life, adrenaline still coursing through her veins. She found herself on the darkened street, looking back only once, catching a glimpse of the light through the windows, wondering what would happen next. She made her way back to her car, her mind racing with a mix of fear and confusion. As she drove away, the tension in her chest began to ease, but her thoughts remained scattered. She reached her house, locked the doors, and collapsed onto her bed, exhaustion taking over. Despite her efforts to stay awake, her eyes closed, and she drifted into a restless sleep filled with fragmented images of Jake.

She had done it; she had stopped him, but Abi realized the darkness that had taken him was still out there, waiting and hungry, and it would come for her next.

* * *

Abi woke to the sound of her phone buzzing incessantly. The morning light streamed through her window, and for a moment, she struggled to remember where she was. Then, the events of the previous night came rushing back, and a wave of anxiety washed over her.

She sat up, reaching for her phone on the bedside table. The clock read 6:45 a.m. Several missed calls and texts filled the screen. Her hand shook slightly as she opened a message from Megan, her friend from the studio:

OMG! Did you hear about Jake? Where are you? The police are at the studio! Something happened last night. They say he's missing or worse, maybe dead??

Abi stared at the message, her mind racing. Jake—missing or possibly dead? A chill ran through her as a flood of questions filled her thoughts. *What had happened after I escaped? Did the police find any trace of me being there?* She needed to be careful, but more than that, she needed to find out what had happened at Jake's house.

She forced herself to focus, to push through the confusion and fear. She needed to go to the studio, to find out what had happened, and, more importantly, what they knew. Her thoughts flashed back to the previous night—the fight, the light, the device. She hadn't intended to kill him, but the device had acted on its own, unleashing a power she couldn't control. She dressed quickly, her hands trembling as she pulled on her clothes. Her mind was a blur, but one thing was certain: she had to be careful. The town would be stunned by the news of Jake's possible death, and she couldn't afford any mistakes.

As she drove to the studio, Abi's thoughts returned to the device. It was still in Jake's house, still dormant, but she couldn't leave it there. She needed to retrieve it, to find a way to understand what it was and how to use it.

Abi arrived at the studio to find a scene of chaos. Police cars were parked haphazardly around the building, their lights flashing. A small crowd had gathered outside, whispering anxiously among themselves. Abi parked a short distance away and walked toward the entrance. She spotted a familiar face in the crowd, Megan, one of the assistant producers, and hurried over to her.

"What happened?" Abi asked, trying to keep her voice steady.

Megan turned, her face pale. "Abi! Thank God you're here. It's Jake... they found signs of a struggle at his house this morning, but they can't find him anywhere. They're saying it might have been some kind of accident, but..." Her voice trailed off, trembling.

Abi's stomach tightened. "But what?"

Megan glanced around nervously, then lowered her voice. "Some of the crew... they said they heard something last night, after we all left. Lights flickering, strange noises, and then the way things were left at his place... it doesn't look like an accident, Abi."

Abi swallowed hard, trying to process the information. "Did they say anything about what might have caused it?"

Megan shook her head. "Not yet. The police are still investigating, but... it doesn't feel right. Something's wrong."

Abi nodded. She had to get to Jake's house, had to retrieve the device before anyone else discovered it, but she wasn't sure how. The house would be crawling with investigators by now. She was about to say something when a voice called out from behind her.

"Abi! Over here!"

She turned to see Sheriff Roy Thompson, a grizzled man in his fifties and lead investigator on the case, making his way toward her. He was a tall, broad-shouldered man with a stern expression, his eyes sharp and calculating.

"Sheriff," Abi greeted him, forcing a smile. "I just heard the news. This is… it's terrible."

"It is. I'm sorry to have to drag you into this, Abi, but we need to ask you some questions. You were close to Jake, weren't you?"

Her heart jumped; she had to be careful. "Yes, I worked with him for years. We were good friends."

Thompson studied her for a moment. "I understand this is a difficult time, but anything you can tell us would be helpful. Did Jake seem different to you recently? Acting strange, anything out of the ordinary?"

Abi hesitated, thinking. She had to tread carefully. "He… he was under a lot of stress," she said slowly. "The show, the pressure, it was getting to him. But I never imagined anything like this would happen."

Thompson nodded, his expression thoughtful. "We're still piecing things together, but from what we've gathered so far, there were signs of a struggle at Jake's house. We're treating this as a potential crime scene. Until we know more, we can't rule anything out."

"You think something… happened to him?"

Thompson's gaze was steady. "We're not ruling anything out at this point. I'll need you to come down to the station later for a more, well, formal interview. For now, try to think of anything that might help us understand what happened, anything at all."

"Of course, Sheriff. I'll do whatever I can."

Thompson gave her a curt nod and walked away, leaving Abi standing in the midst of the chaos, her mind spinning. She had to get to that device, but she was still unclear what to do after that. Surrounded by the whispers and the flashing lights, Abi felt the weight of the situation bearing down on her. She had unleashed something, and now it was up to her to try and stop it.

Chapter 8

Abi spent the rest of the day in a state of shock, struggling with the events that had transpired. She had barely escaped Jake's house with her life, and now he was missing, or dead. But what gripped her most was the fear that he wasn't gone at all, that somehow, the darkness still lingered, waiting for another chance to strike.

Her phone buzzed again with a message, another crew member asking about Jake, wondering if she'd heard anything new. She wished she had answers, but there were only more questions. Abi knew she needed to act quickly. She sensed that Jake was still out there, and far from finished with her or Evergreen.

By the time she made it back to her small apartment, her thoughts were a tangled mess of fear, guilt, and confusion. But she couldn't rest, not yet. She had to think, had to plan her next move. The police were now involved, and it was only a matter of time before they discovered the device in Jake's house. If that happened, there would be questions, questions she wasn't prepared to answer. And worse, the evil that had taken over Jake was still inside him, growing stronger.

Abi sat on the edge of her bed, staring blankly at the wall as her mind churned. She knew she had to return to Jake's house; there was no other option. That *thing* was the key to understanding what had happened, but it was also a danger. She had to be careful. She wasn't a thief or a criminal. She knew she needed help; the thought was a lifeline, and she latched onto it desperately. She couldn't do this alone. There was only one person she could think of, someone she hadn't spoken to in years, but who might be able to help her. It was a long shot, but she was running out of options.

She picked up her phone and hesitated, her finger hovering over the contact list. Then, with a deep breath, she scrolled through the names until she found the one she was looking for: Chris Carter.

Chris had been a friend of hers in college, back when they were both studying journalism. They had drifted apart after graduation, with Chris pursuing a career in investigative reporting while Abi had ended up in television production. Chris had always been tenacious, fearless in the face of danger, and if anyone could help her, it was him.

Abi pressed the call button, feeling anxious as she waited for the line to connect. It rang several times before a voice answered, a bit out of sorts and clearly caught off guard. "Abi? Is that you?"

In that instant, as Abi listened to the familiar voice on the other end of the line, she couldn't help but remember their history. Chris had always been there for her, even when she hadn't asked for it. In college, he had been her constant companion, her protector, always watching out for her, always ready to step in when things got tough. She knew he cared for her deeply, perhaps more than she had ever been comfortable acknowledging. There had been moments when she caught glimpses of that longing in his eyes, a hope that she had never been able to return. Chris had once told her, in a rare moment of vulnerability, that he would always be there for her, no matter what. Back then, she had smiled and brushed it off, not realizing how serious he had been. Now, years later, she felt the weight of his promise. Would he drop everything and come to her aid simply because she asked? She was about to find out.

"Chris, I need your help," she blurted out, the words tumbling over each other in her rush to explain. "Something... something terrible has happened, and I don't know who else to turn to."

There was a pause on the other end, and then Chris' voice became more alert. "What's going on? Are you okay?"

"No, I'm not okay. Jake Walker. He's dead, Chris. But that's not the worst of it. There's something else, something I don't understand, but it's dangerous, and I'm scared."

"Slow down," Chris said, his tone calming but urgent. "Tell me what happened."

Abi took another deep breath and began to explain, recounting the events of the past few weeks, the changes in Jake, the incident at the studio, and finally, the confrontation at his house. She left nothing out, telling Chris about the device, the darkness that had consumed Jake, and her fear that it was still out there, waiting to strike again. When she finished, there was a long silence on the other end of the line.

"Chris?" Abi whispered, fear gnawing at her.

"I'm here .This... this is serious, Abi. You're sure about everything you've told me?"

"Absolutely, I saw it with my own eyes. I don't know what that thing is, but it's powerful, and it's dangerous, and now the police are involved, and I don't know what to do."

Chris sighed. "Okay, listen. I'm going to catch the next flight out there. We'll figure this out together, but you have to promise me you'll be careful. Don't go near Jake's house until I get there. The police will be watching, and we can't afford to make any mistakes."

"I promise. Just please hurry, Chris. I don't know how much time we have."

"I'll be there as soon as I can. Stay safe, Abi. We'll get through this."

Abi ended the call and set the phone down. Help was on the way, but time was running out. She had to be ready.

* * *

Chris arrived the next morning, looking tired but determined. They met at a small diner on the outskirts of Evergreen, far enough from prying eyes. Abi felt a surge of relief at the sight of him, a familiar face in the midst of the chaos.

"Abi," Chris said as he embraced her. "You look like you haven't slept in days."

"I haven't. I've been too afraid. Every time I close my eyes, I see Jake… or whatever he is now."

"We need to figure out what's going on and fast. The first step is to get that device before anyone else finds it," he said.

"But how? The police are watching the house. I can't just walk in and take it."

"I have a plan. We're going to need a distraction, something that will draw the police away long enough for us to get in and grab it. Do you know if there's anyone on the force you can trust? Someone who might look the other way?"

She hesitated, then shook her head. "No, I don't know any of them well enough to ask for that kind of favor."

Chris frowned. "Okay, we'll do this the hard way. We'll create a distraction ourselves. But first, we need to scope out the place, see what we're dealing with."

Abi agreed, and after discussing their plan at the diner, they decided to wait until nightfall to approach Jake's house. As darkness settled over Evergreen, they drove to a spot just beyond Jake's property, parking a safe distance away. The house looked as nondescript as ever, but there were police cars stationed nearby, and a few officers could be seen patrolling the area. Chris observed the scene carefully, then turned to Abi.

"Here's what we're going to do. I'm going to create a diversion, something that will draw their attention away from the house. When that happens, you're going to slip inside and grab the thing. Be quick, be quiet, and get out as fast as you can. Got it?"

Abi nodded. "What kind of diversion?"

"Don't worry about that. Just be ready when the time

comes."

This was it, the moment of truth. If they succeeded, they might have a chance to stop whatever was happening. If they failed… She didn't want to think about that.

Chris got out of the car. Abi watched as he moved stealthily toward the police cars, disappearing in the dark. Minutes ticked by, each one feeling like an eternity, until suddenly, there was a loud crash, followed by shouting. She jumped, then saw the police officers rushing toward the source of the commotion. Whatever Chris had done, it was working. This was her chance.

She slipped out of the car, her movements quick and quiet as she approached Jake's house. The door was still unlocked, just as it had been the night before, and she went inside, closing it gently behind her.

The house was silent, the air thick with the weight of the previous night's events. Abi moved toward the living room, her heart pounding. As she stepped into the room, she noticed the blanket was still partially covering it, but it looked as if it had been moved, slightly shifted from where she remembered it. She was surprised that the police—or anyone else—hadn't found the device yet. She grabbed it, feeling the cold metal in her hands. For a moment, she hesitated, feeling the strange energy run through her, but she forced herself to move, to get out before it was too late. As she turned to leave, she heard a sound that made her blood run cold. A low, guttural growl echoed through the room, followed by the sound of footsteps, heavy footsteps, coming from the hallway.

Abi froze. She had no idea who, or what, was in the house with her, but she knew one thing for certain, she needed to get out, now. She clutched it tightly and bolted for the front door, her footsteps echoing loudly in the empty house. The growl grew louder, more menacing, but she didn't dare look back.

She reached the door and yanked it open, throwing herself outside just as something large and heavy crashed into the wall behind her. Abi ran, breathing hard, as she sprinted toward the car where Chris was waiting. She could hear the sound of pursuit behind her, but she didn't stop, didn't look back. She had the egg-shaped device, and that was all that mattered. She reached the car and threw open the door, diving inside just as Chris hit the gas. The tires squealed as they sped away, leaving the house and whatever was inside it behind.

Abi collapsed in the passenger seat, clutching the device to her chest as she struggled to catch her breath.

"What happened?" Chris asked.

"I… I don't know. There was something in the house, something… not human I think, but I got it."

Chris' eyes questioned her remark, but answered. "Good. Now we need to figure out what to do with it."

Abi stared at it. The power it held was dangerous, unpredictable. They couldn't keep it, but they couldn't destroy it either, not without knowing what they were dealing with.

"There's someone I know," Chris said. "An old friend, someone who might be able to help us. He's… a little different, but if anyone can figure out what this thing is, it's him."

Abi nodded, trusting Chris' judgment. She had come this far, and there was no turning back now. "Let's go," she said, her voice steady despite the fear gnawing at her insides. "We need answers."

Chris agreed and stepped on the gas; the car sped away from Evergreen and into the unknown.

* * *

They drove for hours, the landscape outside the car windows shifting from small-town familiarity to the vast, empty stretches of rural Missouri. The tension between them was thick, both of them too lost in their thoughts to make much conversation.

Abi ran her fingers along the top of the device, tracing the smooth, alien surface. The hum of the engine and the drone of the tires on the road faded into the background as her thoughts turned inward. The events of the past few days replayed in her mind like a broken record, and each time she revisited them, the sense of dread grew. *What have we gotten ourselves into?*

As they crossed into the outskirts of Kansas City, Chris finally broke the silence. "We're almost there."

Abi looked up, her thoughts snapping back to the present. The road signs indicated they were approaching an industrial area on the edge of the city, a place that looked deserted and foreboding in the dim light of early evening. "Where are we going?"

"An old warehouse," Chris replied. "It's off the grid, so to speak. My friend uses it as a lab of sorts. He's not exactly a people person, but he knows more about this kind of thing than anyone I've ever met."

Abi wasn't entirely reassured, but she was willing to follow Chris' lead. She didn't have any other options.

They pulled up to a large, unmarked building, its exterior weathered and covered in graffiti. Chris parked the car, and they both sat there for a moment, gathering their thoughts before stepping out into the cool evening air. The warehouse loomed above them, its windows dark and empty. Chris led the way to a side door, knocking in a pattern that seemed to be some sort of code. After a few tense moments, the door opened, and a figure emerged from the shadows.

"Chris," the man said. "You're late."

"We ran into some trouble," he said, gesturing to

Abi. "This is Abi. We need your help, Mark."

Mark stepped aside to let them in, his sharp eyes assessing Abi as she passed. He was a tall, wiry man with a grizzled beard and a scar running down the side of his face, giving him a vaguely ominous appearance. But there was an intelligence in his gaze that made Abi feel like he was seeing right through her.

"So, this is it?" Mark asked, nodding toward the object in Abi's hands as he closed the door behind them.

"Yes. It's… it's dangerous. It killed Jake," she said.

Mark's eyes filled with curiosity as he subtly gestured for them to follow him.

"Let's take a look, then." He led them through a labyrinth of corridors until they reached a large, open space filled with an assortment of equipment, computers, and workbenches. The air was dense with the smell of metal and chemicals, and the faint buzz of electricity filled the air. Mark cleared a space on one of the workbenches and gestured for Abi to set the device down. She carefully placed it on the cold, steel surface.

Mark studied it for a long moment, his expression unreadable. He reached out to touch it, but stopped just short, his hand hovering above the surface. "Interesting," he muttered. "Very interesting."

"What is it?" Chris asked.

Mark didn't answer right away. Instead, he walked

over to a shelf and retrieved a set of tools, laying them out on the bench with methodical precision. "This is like nothing I've ever seen before, but it's not completely unfamiliar, either."

Abi and Chris exchanged a glance, both of them curious.

"What do you mean?" Abi asked.

Mark picked up a small scanner and ran it over the surface of the device. The screen lit up with a series of numbers and symbols, none of which made any sense to Abi.

"The design, the materials... they're not from Earth, at least not any known source, but it's more than that. This thing is ancient, thousands, maybe tens of thousands of years old."

"How is that possible?" she asked.

Mark shook his head, his eyes still fixed on it. "It's not, at least not by any conventional understanding. This thing, it's a relic, but it's also alive in some way. It's a machine, but it's also... something more..." he said, trailing off. He scratched his head, deep in thought while his eyes continued to study it in bewilderment.

Chris frowned, clearly disturbed by Mark's words. "And what about Jake? What did it do to him?"

Mark's expression darkened. "If I had to guess, I'd

say it has some kind of… consciousness, or maybe it's a conduit for something else. When Jake came into contact with it, it merged with him, changed him on a fundamental level. It used him as a host, a vessel for whatever it was trying to accomplish."

Abi's stomach churned at the thought. "And now?"

Mark set down the scanner and looked at them both, his gaze intense. "Now, it's dormant. The energy it used to merge with Jake is spent, at least for the moment. But it's not destroyed, not by a long shot. This thing, it's waiting. For what, I don't know, but if it were to find another host…" He trailed off again, letting the implications hang in the air.

Abi shuddered. "We need to destroy it."

Mark shook his head. "It's not that simple. Whatever this thing is, it's beyond our ability to understand, let alone destroy. If we're not careful, we could make things worse."

"Then what do we do?" Chris asked.

Mark was silent for a long moment, as if he were trying to unravel its secrets by sheer force of will. "There's one possibility," he finally said. "We could try to neutralize it, contain it somehow. But it would require specialized equipment, and even then, there's no guarantee it would work."

"What kind of equipment?" Abi asked.

Mark, reluctant to share too much, "There's a facility, a research lab, up north. It's highly classified. I've worked with them before, on other... unconventional projects. If anyone can help us, it's them."

Chris' posture straightened, "You're talking about the government, aren't you? Black ops, secret experiments, the kind of place where people disappear?"

"It's a risk, but it's the only option I can think of. If we don't do something, this thing could cause untold damage," Mark explained.

Abi rubbed her temples. Everything was happening so fast, and the stakes were higher than she could have ever imagined. However, she knew Mark was right. They couldn't just leave it where it was, and they couldn't destroy it. They had to try to contain it, even if it meant putting their lives on the line. "Let's do it," she said, her voice firm. "Whatever it takes, we have to stop this thing."

Chris nodded. "We're in this together. Just tell us what we need to do."

"I'll make the arrangements," Mark said. "But it's going to take some time. We'll need to be careful, and if word gets out, it could attract all kinds of unwanted attention."

Abi pushed her nerves aside, knowing this was what needed to be done in order to save Jake, if she still could. They had come too far to back down now. "Thank you

Mark," her voice steady. "We'll do whatever it takes."

"Then let's get to work. We have a long road ahead of us, and we can't afford to make any mistakes."

The next few days were a blur of preparation and tension. Mark worked tirelessly to secure the necessary equipment and contacts, while Abi and Chris tried to keep a low profile, avoiding the police and anyone else who might be looking for them.

Abi could feel the weight of the device in her thoughts, even when she wasn't holding it. It was as if it had wormed its way into her mind, whispering dark thoughts and fears that she couldn't forget. She knew it was dangerous, knew it had the power to destroy everything in its path, but she also felt a strange, almost magnetic pull toward it, a curiosity that frightened her as much as it intrigued her.

Chris seemed to sense Abi's anxiety and tried to keep her focused on the task at hand. He was a steady presence, his calm demeanor a reassuring counterbalance to the chaos swirling around them. Even he couldn't hide the strain of the situation, and Abi could see the worry etched into his features. Finally, after what felt like an eternity of waiting, Mark called them to the warehouse.

"It's time," he said. "Everything's in place. We leave tonight."

Abi tensed as they gathered the few belongings they

would need for the journey. The plan was simple enough—they would drive north under the cover of darkness, avoiding major roads and staying out of sight. Once they reached the facility, Mark would use his contacts to gain access, and they would hand it over to the scientists there, who would attempt to neutralize it. It was a risky plan, and there were countless things that could go wrong, but they had no other choice.

As night fell, they loaded it into the back of a nondescript van that Mark had acquired. Abi climbed into the passenger seat while Mark started the engine, and Chris slid the side door shut and settled in the back. "Are you ready for this?" Mark asked.

She nodded, though she wasn't sure if she was answering him or trying to convince herself. "Let's go."

* * *

The dark landscape passed by in a blur as they sped toward their destination. Just the engine and the occasional murmur of conversation between Mark and Chris as they discussed the route could be heard.

Abi stared out the window, her mind churning with a thousand thoughts. But, the most disturbing thought of all was the nagging fear that the darkness had already found another host, one they didn't even know about.

They drove for hours, the night deepening around

them as they left the city behind and entered the remote wilderness of northern Missouri. The roads became narrower, more winding, and the trees closed in around them, their branches forming a dark canopy overhead.

Finally, just as the first light of dawn began to creep over the horizon, they arrived at the facility. It was an ordinary building, hidden deep within the woods and surrounded by a tall, barbed-wire fence. There were no signs, no markings to indicate what it was, but the presence of armed guards at the gate made it clear that this was no ordinary research lab.

Mark pulled up to the gate and flashed a badge at the guard, who nodded and opened the gate without a word. They drove through and parked in front of the building, the tension in the van thick enough to cut with a knife. "Stay close," Mark said as they stepped out of the van. "We're not out of this yet."

Abi and Chris, with Chris carrying the device, followed Mark as he led them toward the entrance. The guards watched them closely, their expressions unreadable behind what looked like tactical helmets with dark-tinted visors, maybe even equipped with night vision.

Inside, the facility was cold and sterile, the walls lined with metal and glass. They were met by a man in a white lab coat, his expression serious as he motioned for them to follow him. "We've been expecting you," the man said, his voice clipped and efficient. "This way."

They were led down a series of corridors, the air growing colder and more oppressive with each step. Abi felt her chest tighten as they approached a large, reinforced door at the end of the hallway. The scientist pressed a series of buttons on a control panel, and the door slid open with a hiss, revealing a large, circular room filled with machinery and monitors. "This is our containment chamber," the scientist explained as they stepped inside. "It's designed to isolate and neutralize anomalous objects. Once it's inside, we'll begin the process of deactivation."

Abi's eyes locked on the containment chamber in the center of the room. It was a large, cylindrical structure made of thick, transparent material, with a series of metal restraints and cables extending from its sides.

"Place it on the platform," the scientist instructed.

Chris carefully set the device on the platform, setting it down with a reverence that bordered on fear. The scientist activated a series of controls, and the platform began to rise, lifting it into the containment chamber. The metal restraints clicked into place, securing it as the chamber's walls closed around it.

Abi watched, damn near holding her breath, as the scientist began the deactivation process. The monitors came to life, displaying a series of complex readings and data streams that made no sense to her. But something was wrong. The hum of the device became louder, vibrating through the chamber walls as if it were alive. The monitors began to flash red, warning lights blinking as the readings spiked.

"What's happening?" she asked.

The scientist's expression was disturbed as he typed furiously at the controls. "It's resisting containment. It's… it's adapting."

Abi's heart raced as she watched the device, its surface pulsing with a dark, ominous light. The metal restraints groaned under the strain, and the containment chamber began to vibrate violently.

"We need to shut it down!" Chris shouted.

The scientist shook his head, sweat beading on his forehead. "It's too late. It's… "

There was a deafening crack, and the containment chamber shattered, the force of the explosion sending them all crashing to the floor.

Abi's vision blurred as she tried to scramble to her feet, her ears ringing from the blast. The room was filled with smoke and debris, and she could barely make out the shape of the device in the center of the chaos, still pulsing with that dark, malevolent light.

Chris grabbed her arm, pulling her to her feet as they stumbled toward the exit. "We have to get out of here!"

Abi's gaze turned to the device. Without thinking, she

lunged toward it and scooped it up, its weight surprisingly light in her hands.

Before they could reach the door, a cold, unnatural voice filled the room, freezing them in their tracks. "You cannot escape."

Abi's blood ran cold as she turned to face the source of the voice. The device was now pulsing in her hands, its surface rippling and shifting like a living thing. As they watched in horror, the energy from the device appeared to draw out something from the air, distorting it into a vague, humanoid shape, dark and foreboding. Jake's voice seemed to come from everywhere, echoing with a distorted timbre. "You thought you could contain me? You thought you could destroy me?"

Abi felt a surge of terror as the figure's gaze locked onto her, its eyes glowing.

"You are nothing," it hissed. "You are insignificant."

Chris stepped forward, placing himself between Abi and the figure. "Stay back!"

The figure tilted its head, "You cannot stop me, or what is coming." The figure lunged at them, its form shifting and warping as it reached out with elongated, clawed hands.

Chris shoved Abi to the side, taking the brunt of the impact as the figure slammed into him, sending them both crashing to the floor.

"Chris!" Abi screamed, clutching the device tightly as she scrambled to her feet, trying to reach him.

The figure was too fast. It wrapped its clawed hands around Chris' throat, lifting him off the ground with inhuman strength, squeezing. Abi watched in horror as Chris' face turned blue, his eyes bulging as he struggled to breathe. She had to do something, had to stop it, but she was unable to move. Suddenly the figure released him, dropping him to the floor like a discarded toy. Chris gasped for air, clutching his throat, trying to crawl away, but the figure was already turning its attention back to Abi.

"You will not escape," it said, its voice cold and final.

Abi backed away with the device, trying to think of a way out, but there was nowhere to go. The figure was too powerful, too fast, and she was out of options.

The figure stepped toward her, its clawed hands reaching out as its eyes glowed. Then, just as it was about to strike, a loud, metallic clang echoed through the room, followed by a blinding flash of light. Abi shielded her eyes as she tried to make sense of what was happening. The figure let out a scream of rage and pain, its form fluttering and distorted as it staggered back. When the light faded, Abi saw Mark standing near the entrance, holding a large, industrial grade taser.

"Get out of here!" he yelled.

Abi didn't need to be told twice. She rushed to Chris'

side, helping him to his feet as they made a desperate dash for the exit. The figure was still staggering from the attack, its form flickering like a malfunctioning hologram. As they reached the door, it let out a furious roar, the sound reverberating through the facility as the walls shook.

"Run!" Mark shouted, firing the taser again as the figure lunged toward them.

They didn't look back. Abi and Chris ran as fast as they could, the sound of the figure's enraged screams echoing in their ears as they fled the facility and burst out into the open air. They didn't stop running until they reached the van and then collapsed inside. "What... what was that?" Abi gasped.

Chris shook his head, his face pale and drawn. "I don't know, definitely not human."

Mark appeared at the driver's side. "We need to get out of here now. That thing, whatever it is, won't stay down for long."

They had no idea what they were dealing with, but one thing was clear, they were outmatched. As the van sped away from the facility, Abi realized that they had only just begun to uncover the true horror of what they were facing. The device was a catalyst, a trigger for the darkness that now inhabited Jake. Now, that something was awake.

Chapter 9

The van traveled down the empty highway, the early morning light illuminated the desolate landscape. The tension inside the vehicle was undeniable, a thick, suffocating silence hanging in the air as they tried to process everything. Abi sat in the back seat, staring out the window with unseeing eyes, her mind still replaying the encounter with the dark force that had merged with Jake.

Chris was slumped in the passenger seat, his breath shallow as he clutched his bruised throat. Mark was behind the wheel, sullen, as he navigated the winding roads with a steady hand. None of them spoke, the weight of their situation pressing down on them.

Abi's thoughts were all over the place. The dark force that had taken over Jake was unlike anything she had ever imagined.

"We can't outrun it," Chris finally rasped, breaking the heavy silence. His voice was hoarse, barely more than a whisper, but the urgency in his words was unmistakable. "That *thing*... it's not going to stop."

Abi's voice trembled as she spoke. "The police think Jake is dead, but they haven't found a body. He's just... gone."

Chris turned his head, concern etched on his face. "So, he's missing? Or worse, still out there?"

Abi nodded. "I don't think it's over. Whatever he is now... it's still out there, somewhere."

"Then we need to assume it's not gone for good, that it's still out there, plotting. We're dealing with something far beyond our understanding," Mark said.

Chris took a deep breath, wincing. "If Jake's missing, then it means whatever's left of him—whatever he became—is still out there, looking for something. Maybe the device, maybe us."

Mark nodded, "And that makes this even more urgent. We don't just have to worry about stopping that thing; we have to make sure it can't find us or use the device against us."

Abi shuddered at the thought. "We don't even know if he's alive or... something else entirely. But whatever he is now, he's dangerous, and he's not going to stop."

Chris nodded. "And if the police find him first, or if he shows up in Evergreen... things could get even worse. We need to act before that happens."

Abi turned away from the window. "But how? We couldn't even contain it, let alone destroy it. What can we possibly do against something like that?"

"There has to be a way," Mark said, more to himself than to anyone else. "We just need to figure out what we're dealing with."

"Do you think he's following us?' Chris asked, glancing nervously out the back window, half-expecting to see Jake in pursuit.

"I don't know, but we can't take any chances. We need to get as far away from here as possible."

Abi felt a surge of panic rising. "Where are we supposed to go? There's no place we can hide from something like that."

Mark was silent for a moment, considering their options. "We're not going to hide. We're going to find out what that thing is and how to stop it. I hate to say it based on what just happened, but there's someone else I know, an expert in ancient artifacts and the paranormal. I *do* believe he can help us."

"Another one of your secret contacts?" Chris said.

"I know, but he's a former colleague. We've worked

together on some projects in the past. If we can find him, he might have better answers."

Abi didn't know what to think, but the faint hope that Mark's contact might hold the key to helping Jake made her ask, "Where is he?"

"Last I heard, he was in New Mexico, but he moves around a lot. We'll have to track him down."

"New Mexico?" Chris echoed. "That's halfway across the country. We'll never make it in time."

"We don't have a choice," Mark said. "If we stay here, we're as good as dead. We have to keep moving, stay ahead of that thing. It's our only chance."

Abi thought of traveling that far, all while being pursued by that thing, was almost too much to bear, but she knew Mark was right. They couldn't stay in one place; they had to keep moving, keep fighting, no matter how hopeless it seemed. "Okay," she said, "Let's do it."

Mark pushed the accelerator of the van a little harder, putting as much distance between themselves and the facility as possible.

As the miles passed, the landscape gradually changed from the dense forests of Missouri to the flat, open plains of the Midwest. The sun climbed higher in the sky, casting a harsh, unforgiving light over the desolate landscape. Abi tried to focus on the road ahead and hoped that they might find a way to stop whatever it was before it was too late.

But, even as she tried to keep her thoughts focused, she had a feeling of dread that had taken root deep inside her. That thing was still out there, and it was only a matter of time before it caught up to them.

Hours passed in silence, with only the sound of the road as they barreled down the highway. Abi's eyelids grew heavy, the exhaustion of the past few days finally catching up to her. She fought to stay awake, but the rhythmic motion of the van and the monotony of the landscape lulled her into a fitful sleep.

She was jolted awake by the sudden blare of a horn. Her eyes flew open, and she saw that they were now on a busy interstate, surrounded by trucks and cars as they weaved through traffic. Mark, still gripping the steering wheel tight.

"What's going on?" Abi asked, still sleepy.

Mark didn't take his eyes off the road. "We're getting close to the state line. I wanted to get as far as possible before we stopped to rest."

Abi rubbed her eyes, erasing the lingering fog of sleep. Chris was still slumped in the passenger seat, his eyes closed as he tried to get some rest. The tension in the van had lessened, but not completely, a constant reminder of the danger they were in.

As they continued to drive, the landscape began to change again, the flat plains giving way to rolling hills and jagged rocky outcroppings. The sun was beginning to set, turning the sky a deep shade of orange.

"We'll stop at the next town," Mark said, breaking the silence. "We need to get some rest and refuel again. We're running on fumes."

Abi stretched, her body aching from hours of sitting in the van. Chris was visibly uncomfortable also, stirring in his seat.

The interstate eventually led them to a small, dusty town tucked between low hills and red sandstone cliffs. It was a forgotten place, with a few gas stations, a diner, and a rundown motel that looked like it hadn't seen a visitor in years. Mark pulled into the gas station, the van sputtering as it came to a stop next to the pump.

Chris woke, looking around. "Where are we?"

"Somewhere in New Mexico. We'll fill up here and grab something to eat. We can rest for a few hours before we hit the road again."

Abi and Chris followed Mark into the gas station, the bell above the door jangling as they entered. The interior was dimly lit and smelled faintly of grease and stale coffee. A bored-looking attendant stood behind the counter.

Mark paid for the gas and grabbed a few bottles of water and some snacks from the shelves. After they had refueled, Mark drove the van across the street to the motel. The neon sign blinked weakly, casting a sickly green light over the cracked pavement.

Abi felt a shiver run down her spine as she stared at the rundown building. It looked like the kind of place where bad things happened, the kind of place where people disappeared and were never heard from again. "Are you sure this is a good idea?"

"It's the only place for miles," Mark replied, his tone matter-of-fact. "We don't have much choice."

Reluctantly, she followed him and Chris into the motel office, where an elderly man sat behind the desk, watching an old black-and-white television. He barely acknowledged them as Mark paid for a room, handing over several crumpled bills.

"Room seven," the man muttered, sliding a tarnished key across the counter. "Down the hall."

They found the room at the end of a dimly lit corridor, the walls lined with faded floral wallpaper that had seen better days. Mark pushed the door open, revealing a small, dingy room with two beds and a worn-out chair. Abi set her bag down on the bed closest to the door, her body protesting with every movement. The room was stuffy and smelled faintly of mildew, but it was a place to rest, and for that, she was grateful.

"We'll take turns keeping watch," Mark said. "We can't risk letting our guard down."

Chris agreed, already pulling a chair over to the window where he could keep an eye on the parking lot. Abi knew that sleep would be difficult, but she was so exhausted that she couldn't help but collapse onto the bed, her body sinking into the lumpy mattress. Despite her concerns, sleep claimed her quickly, dragging her down into a deep, dreamless oblivion.

* * *

Abi came to with a gasp, as she struggled to remember where she was. The room was dark, the only light coming from the glow of the neon sign outside the window. She could hear the steady breathing of the guys, both of them fast asleep. For a moment, she allowed herself to believe that everything was normal, that the events of the past few days had been nothing more than a nightmare. But as her mind cleared, the reality of their situation came crashing back down on her, and the fear returned with a vengeance. She sat up in bed, her eyes scanning the room for any signs of danger. Everything was still, the only sound was the soft whir of the air conditioner as it struggled to keep the room cool.

She glanced at the clock on the nightstand. It was just after three in the morning, the darkest part of the night when everything seemed more threatening. She slipped out of bed, careful not to wake the others, and quietly made her way to the window. Chris had left the chair positioned in front of it, and Abi sat down, staring out at the empty parking lot.

The town was quiet, the streets deserted. There was something unsettling about the stillness, as if the entire place had been abandoned, left to decay under the weight of its own neglect. Abi's thoughts turned to Jake and the way he had changed, how his eyes had burned with a strange light, and how he seemed to be channeling something dark. All of the answers to her questions seemed out of reach, like fragments of a dream that slipped away the moment she tried to grasp them. But one thing was clear—it was old, powerful, and filled with an intelligence that defied understanding. And, most importantly, it was after them.

She stared out into the night, every shadow seeming to shift and move with a life of its own. She could feel its presence, lurking just beyond the edge of her vision, waiting for the right moment to strike. She was so lost in her thoughts that she almost didn't notice the figure standing at the far end of the parking lot, partially obscured by the shadows. Abi focused on the figure. It was tall, its form indistinct in the dim light, the way it seemed to be watching her.

She reached out to wake Chris, but before her hand could make contact, the figure stepped out of the shadows, moving into the light cast by the flickering neon sign. It was a man. Abi blinked in surprise, now confused. The man was dressed in a long coat, his hat pulled low over his eyes, and he was carrying a large duffel bag slung over one shoulder. He stopped in the middle of the parking lot, looking directly at the motel room. Abi's breath hitched as their eyes met. There was something about the man, something she couldn't quite place. He seemed out of place in the rundown town, like a ghost from a different era, passing through on his way to someplace else.

For some time, they stared at each other, the distance between them seeming to shrink as the seconds ticked by. And then, without a word, the man walked away.

Abi sat frozen in place, her mind struggling to process what she had just seen. She knew she should wake the others, tell them about the stranger in the parking lot, but something held her back, a nagging feeling that the man wasn't a threat, that he was something else entirely. The thought made her shiver, and she pulled her knees up to her chest, wrapping her arms around them. Sleep was out of reach now, her thoughts refusing to let go.

The hours passed slowly, the night gradually giving way to the pale light of dawn. Abi kept her vigil at the window, her eyes heavy with exhaustion, but her mind too restless to let her sleep.

When the first rays of sunlight began to creep over the horizon, she finally allowed herself to relax, the tension in her muscles easing as the darkness retreated. Chris stirred on the bed, blinking as he sat up. "Morning already?" he muttered, rubbing his eyes.

Abi nodded. "Yeah. Did you sleep?"

"Barely," Chris admitted, stretching as he tried to work out the kinks in his neck. "What about you?"

"I kept watch," she said, as her gaze drifted back to the now-empty parking lot. "Nothing happened, but…"

"But what?"

Abi hesitated, unsure if she should tell him about the man she had seen. The memory of the stranger's piercing gaze was still fresh in her mind, and she knew she couldn't keep it to herself.

"There was someone in the parking lot last night, a man. He was just… standing there, watching the motel."

"Did he do anything? Try to get in?"

"No. He just stood there for a while, and then he left. But there was something about him… something strange."

"Strange how?"

She struggled to put her feelings into words. "I don't know. It was like… like he didn't belong here. Like he was just passing through, but he knew something we didn't."

"Do you think he's connected to the same life-form? Maybe he's been following us?"

"I don't know," Abi admitted. "But it felt like he was

watching us for a reason."

Chris was silent for a long moment, his gaze drifted to the window as he considered the possibility. "We need to be careful," he finally said. "Whoever he is, we can't let our guard down. We're not safe here."

She realized how vulnerable they were. They were running out of time, out of options, and now there was a new threat, a mysterious stranger who seemed to know more than he was letting on. They needed to find Mark's contact in New Mexico, and fast, but the journey ahead was long, and the risks they faced were growing by the hour.

"We should wake Mark," Chris said, standing up from the bed. "We need to keep moving."

They woke him up from his sleep. He didn't protest as they quickly packed their belongings and left the motel, the sense of urgency driving them forward.

As they climbed back into the van, Abi felt they were being watched, that the man from the parking lot was still out there, somewhere in the shadows, waiting for the right moment to make his move.

They hit the road again, the sun rising behind them as they drove away from the small, forgotten town and toward whatever awaited them. The miles passed, and the landscape changed to the open plains that stretched into the vast deserts of the Southwest. The air grew warmer as they descended, and soon the heat was oppressive, the sun beating down on the van as they traveled along the desolate highways. Abi's mind was a whirlwind of uncertainty, the events of the past few days weighing heavily on her.

As the day wore on, the van began to overheat, the temperature gauge creeping into the red zone. Mark cursed under his breath, pulling over to the side of the road as steam began to billow from under the hood.

"You've got to be shittin' me! We're in the middle of nowhere," Chris said, glancing at the barren landscape around them. "What are we supposed to do now?"

Mark climbed out of the van. He popped the hood and began to inspect the damage. Abi and Chris followed, the heat hitting them like a physical force as they stepped out onto the cracked pavement. The sun was high in the sky, the air shimmering with heat as they stood by the side of the road, the van's engine hissing and sputtering as it cooled down.

"We're miles from the nearest town. We'll have to let it cool down and hope it starts up again. Otherwise, we're stuck."

"That's just great, fuckin' great," Chris muttered.

Abi looked around at the surroundings, feeling hopeless. They couldn't afford to be stranded on this lonely stretch of highway, not with something still out there and the mysterious stranger from the motel possibly following them.

As they waited for the engine to cool, she wandered away from the van, her gaze fixed on the expanse of desert that stretched out before them. The faint rustling of the wind as it swept across the plain was all she could hear. She felt a sense of isolation, a profound loneliness, surrounded by nothing but sand and rock. The world felt vast and empty, as if they were the last people left on Earth. Then, out of the corner of her eye, she saw something, a movement against the distant horizon. She squinted, trying to make out what it was, but the heat waves distorted her vision, making it difficult to see clearly.

"Abi?" Chris called out. "What is it?"

"I saw something, out there, on the horizon."

He frowned, shading his eyes as he looked in the direction she had indicated. "I don't see anything."

"I'm sure I saw something," she insisted. "It was moving."

Mark joined them, scanning the horizon. "Could be a mirage. The heat plays tricks on your eyes out here."

Abi wasn't convinced. There had been something out there, she was sure of it, something that had been watching them.

"Let's get back in the van," Mark said, his tone leaving no room for argument. "We'll wait for the engine to cool down, and then we'll keep moving. We can't stay out here any longer than we have to."

Abi and Chris, both eager to get off the exposed road and away from the open desert, followed. They climbed back into the van, the interior stiflingly hot, but it was a relief to be inside, away from the heat of the sun.

Mark tried the ignition, but the engine refused to turn over, the starter grinding uselessly. He cursed under his breath, slamming his fist against the steering wheel in frustration.

"We're stuck! We'll have to wait for it to cool down completely, and even then, there's no guarantee it'll start."

They were stranded in the middle of nowhere, with no one around for miles. Abi tried to push the anxiety from her mind, but it was like a weight pressing down on her chest, making it difficult to breathe. The minutes ticked by, each one feeling like an eternity as they waited for the engine to cool. The heat inside the van was unforgiving, and Abi felt sweat trickling down her back, her clothes sticking to her skin as she tried to stay calm.

"Maybe we should try calling for help," she suggested, pulling out her phone. She checked the screen and frowned. "No signal... nothing at all," she muttered, shaking the device slightly as if that might change something.

Chris leaned over to look at her phone. "Let me check mine," he said, reaching into his pocket. "Maybe if we step outside, we'll get a better signal." He opened the door and took a step out, holding his phone up toward the sky. Before he could move any further, Mark noticed and quickly intervened.

"What are you doing?"

"Trying to get a signal," Chris replied, confused by Mark's sudden urgency.

Mark shook his head, his face serious. "Turn it off. Both of you, turn your phones off," he insisted.

"Why?" Abi asked.

Mark glanced around the desert, his gaze shifting. "It's actually good they're not working," he said, his voice low. "If something's jamming the signal, it might mean someone—or something—doesn't want us making calls. And if they can block a signal, they can probably track it too. We need to stay off the grid for now… just in case."

Chris hesitated for a moment, then nodded and powered off his phone. Abi did the same, reluctantly.

"So, what do we do?" she asked quietly.

"We wait. Just until we're sure it's safe," Mark said.

Just as she thought she couldn't take the tension any longer, she saw it again, on the horizon, closer this time. "There! I see it again!"

Chris and Mark both looked, their expressions tense as they strained to see what she was pointing at. They saw it too, a dark shape moving against the bright blue sky, growing larger as it approached.

"Get down!" Mark shouted.

They all ducked down in their seats, trying to make themselves as small as possible as the shape grew closer, taking on a more distinct form. It was a man, walking toward them with a deliberate, almost mechanical gait. He was dressed in a long coat, his face obscured by a wide-brimmed hat. Abi recognized him. "It's the man from the motel parking lot."

"What's he doing out here?" Chris whispered.

"I don't know."

"Well, we're not taking any chances. Stay down and stay quiet," Mark said.

They watched in silence as the stranger got closer, his footsteps kicking up small clouds of dust as he walked. He stopped a few feet from the van, his head moved slowly, scanning the area. Abi held her breath, knowing that he could probably hear her heart beating in her chest.

The stranger stood there; his gaze fixed on the van as if he knew they were inside. But then, just as suddenly as he had appeared, he turned and walked away, his figure gradually shrinking into the distance. They waited in silence. Finally, when they were sure he was gone, they allowed themselves to breathe again.

"What the hell was that?" Chris asked.

"I don't know," Mark replied. "But I don't like it. We

need to get this van running and get out of here, fast."

They waited for another hour, the sun beating down on the van, not letting up. Finally, Mark tried the ignition again, and this time, the engine roared to life. They didn't waste any time. He hit the gas, and the van raced down the highway, leaving the desolate stretch of road and the mysterious stranger far behind.

The rest of the drive through New Mexico was tense, but uneventful. They avoided major highways, sticking to back roads and less-traveled routes to avoid being tracked. The landscape shifted from the dry, hot desert air to the more mountainous terrain of New Mexico, the air growing cooler as they climbed higher into the mountains. Mark's contact lived in a remote cabin deep in the woods, far from the prying eyes of the world. It took them hours to navigate the narrow, winding roads that led to the cabin, the dense forest closing in around them as they drove deeper into the wilderness.

By the time they reached the cabin, it was late afternoon, the sun now setting behind the mountains, casting shadows across the forest floor. The cabin was small and unassuming, nestled among the trees with smoke curling lazily from the chimney.

Mark parked the van a short distance away, and they all climbed out, stretching their stiff limbs after the long drive. "This is it. My contact should be inside."

Abi felt a knot of anxiety as they approached the cabin. She had no idea what to expect, whether this contact would be able to help them or if they were walking into another dangerous situation.

Mark knocked on the door, the sound echoing through the silent woods. They waited in silence and listened for any sign of life inside the cabin. Finally, the door opened, and a tall, thin man with wild, unkempt hair and a scraggly beard peered out at them. His eyes were sharp, scanning everyone, assessing them with a shrewd, almost paranoid gaze.

"Mark," the man said, his voice a raspy whisper. "It's been a while."

"Yeah, it has, can we come in? We need your help."

The man hesitated, his gaze lingering on Abi and Chris as if he were trying to see inside their mind. Then, with a reluctant nod, he stepped aside and allowed them to enter.

* * *

The inside of the cabin was cluttered and dimly lit, the walls lined with shelves filled with books, jars of strange substances, and various pieces of old, dusty equipment. The air was thick with the smell of incense and something else, something earthy and musty that Abi couldn't quite place.

The man motioned for them to sit down at a small, rickety table in the center of the room. He didn't offer any refreshments, but Abi was too anxious to notice. She sat down, waiting for the man to speak. Mark was the first to break the silence.

"This is Abi and Chris," Mark gestured towards them. "Guys, this is Walt." Walt nodded his head at them. "We're in serious trouble, and we need your help."

The man studied them, his fingers drumming on the table. "What kind of trouble?"

Abi knew it was up to her to explain. She took a deep breath and began to recount the events of the past few days, the discovery of the device, Jake's transformation, the thing that had emerged from the containment chamber, and the mysterious man who had been following them.

The man listened in silence, his expression unreadable as he absorbed every detail. When Abi finished, he sat back in his chair, staring at the table as if piecing together a puzzle. Finally, he looked up at Abi with an intensity that made her more nervous.

"Well, first off, the stranger you mentioned, sounds like someone from the government—following you, watching you," he said, his tone guarded. "I can't say much more about that, but we need to deal with your problem with the device first. Take care of that, and that little government man will probably disappear."

The room fell into stunned silence, and everyone exchanged uneasy glances, unsure how to react to this new revelation.

"Now, on another note, what you've encountered is something very old, something that predates humanity itself. It's a force, a manifestation of pure malevolence. And, it's not of this world."

"Can we stop it?" Chris asked.

The man shook his head slowly. "You can't stop it, not in the way you're thinking. It's not something that can be killed or destroyed. It's a force of nature, like a storm or an earthquake. You can't destroy a storm, you can only survive it."

Abi's stomach churned. "So what do we do? Just run and hide?"

The man turned his attention to Mark. "You didn't come here just to ask questions, did you? You encountered something, something bad, right?

"We have the device."

"You brought it here? Are you out of your mind?" Walt said, standing up.

"It's the only way. You're the only one who knows how to deal with something like this."

Walt paced back and forth in agitation. "You don't

understand what you're dealing with. The device is a conduit, a source of power. It's not just a machine; it's connected to the dark force now bound to Jake. It amplifies its influence, making it stronger."

"So what do we do? How do we survive this?" Abi asked.

Walt stopped. "There's only one way to survive. You have to sever the connection, destroy the device before it amplifies his power even further, but it won't be easy. The device will resist, and whatever it released will do everything in its power to stop you."

Mark nodded. "We'll do whatever it takes."

Walt, lost in thought, finally said, "There's a place, a place where the device can be destroyed, but it's dangerous, and getting there won't be easy."

"Where is it?" Abi asked.

He took a deep breath, his expression filled with dread. "There's a cave deep in the mountains, a place where the veil between worlds is thin. It's a place of great power. If you can get the device there and destroy it, you might be able to weaken the force that's taken hold of Jake. But be warned, it will fight you every step of the way."

Chris looked at Abi. "We have to try. We can't let that thing stay loose in the world."

"You're right. We have to." Abi looked at Walt with hopeful eyes. They had come too far to back down now. Whatever it took, they would destroy the device and stop the creature before it could unleash any more destruction.

"Very well. I'll help you get there, but after that, you're on your own. I can't go with you, I've already seen too much, but I'll give you what you need to survive the journey," Walt explained.

Mark stood up. "Thank you. We won't forget this."

Walt waved off the thanks and looked out of the window as the last rays of sunlight disappeared behind the mountains. "You'll need to leave at first light, and that *thing* will be hunting you every step of the way. Be careful, and may whatever gods you believe in go with you."

Abi felt the weight of the enormity of the task ahead of them, but she knew they had no choice. If they didn't stop it, no one else would. They would leave at dawn, and by the time the sun set again, they would either have destroyed the device, or they would be dead.

Chapter 10

Jake walked through the streets of Evergreen, his presence now unwelcome. The people who once greeted him with warmth and familiarity averted their eyes, sensing the change in him. He smiled as he passed the hardware store, the corner diner, and the post office—each building holding memories of a life that wasn't truly his. The memories came in fragments, pieces of a puzzle that didn't quite fit. He felt his mind fraying, the darkness within growing stronger, more insistent. Jake noticed how the children no longer followed him, their instincts warning them to keep their distance, and it amused him. Innocence was something he relished, something he could twist and corrupt.

He turned down a narrow alleyway, the shadows closing in around him as he walked. The air was thick with the scent of damp earth and decaying leaves, a smell that seemed to cling to him. He paused in front of a small, dilapidated house at the end of the alley, its windows boarded up and its paint peeling. It was a house that no one in Evergreen had lived in for years, a place that had been forgotten, left to rot in the shadows of the town. But, Jake hadn't forgotten. He could feel the temptation here, the way it seeped into the very walls of the house, calling out to him, urging him to enter.

Jake pushed the door open and stepped inside, the house swallowing him whole. The interior of the house was even more decrepit than the outside, the floors covered in dust and debris, the air stale and suffocating. He moved through the house with purpose, his footsteps echoing in the silence. He knew where he was going, knew what he was looking for. He stopped in front of a large, ornate mirror that hung on the wall in the living room, its surface cracked and dirty. The mirror had once been a beautiful piece, a symbol of wealth and status, but now it was nothing more than a relic of a forgotten time.

He stared at his reflection, studying the face that looked back at him. It was his face, but it wasn't. The lines were too sharp, the eyes a little too dark, the smile too sinister. He reached out and touched the surface of the mirror, his fingers tracing the cracks that marred the glass. The evil inside him stirred, eager and hungry, and he could feel it pushing against the boundaries of his mind, trying to break free.

"Soon," Jake whispered. "Soon, they'll all see."

The mirror seemed to ripple under his touch, the cracks widening, negativity seeping through. Jake could feel the power of the mirror, the way it connected him to this other new part of him, feeding it, amplifying it. He leaned in closer, his breath fogging up the glass as he spoke to the reflection.

"This town is mine," he said with vicious intent. "And they will bow to me, or they will fall."

The reflection in the mirror twisted, the face warping into something monstrous, something that wasn't quite human, but Jake didn't flinch, he welcomed it. This newfound energy surged within him, filling him with a sense of power and control that was intoxicating. He could feel the town slipping further into his grasp, the people unknowingly bending to his will. There was still resistance, still those who hadn't yet succumbed to the fear, and Jake knew that if he were to truly claim Evergreen as his own, he would have to eliminate that problem.

The mirror pulsed with energy, the cracks widening as if it were on the verge of shattering. Jake could see images flickering across the surface—scenes of the townsfolk, of Abi and Chris, and of himself, the creature within him now fully awakened. Then he saw something that made him pause—a vision of Abi standing in a cave, holding the device in her hands. She was surrounded by shadows, her face pale and determined, her eyes filled with fear. Jake studied the vision. "So, that's where you're hiding."

He laughed, a cold, hollow sound that echoed through the empty house. Jake's grip on the mirror tightened, his knuckles turning white as he spoke to the reflection. "You'll never make it," he hissed, getting closer to his reflection. "I'll be waiting for you."

With a final, vicious shove, Jake smashed the mirror with his fist, the glass shattering into a thousand pieces that rained down on the floor. The evil within him swelled, feeding off the destruction, growing stronger, more powerful.

He turned and left the house, his mind focused on one thing, stopping Abi and guaranteeing that the town of Evergreen, and everyone in it, belonged to him. As he walked back through the alley, the shadows seemed to cling to him, swirling around his feet like mist. He could feel his power spreading, seeping into the very heart of the town, infecting everything it touched, and he relished it. Evergreen was his now, and he would stop at nothing to keep it that way.

* * *

Abi, Chris, and Mark were preparing for their final confrontation. The silence was screaming as they gathered their supplies and steeled themselves for the journey ahead. It was the only place where they might have a chance of destroying the device and severing its link to Jake for good. The force within was still out there, and they knew it would do everything in its power to stop them.

Mark led the way through the dense forest, the air cool and crisp, the scent of pine and earth filled their lungs as they continued to climb higher into the mountains. The path was treacherous, the ground uneven and covered in loose rocks that made every step a challenge. Abi felt that they were walking into a trap, that the thing was already waiting for them, hidden in the shadows of the forest, but they had no choice, this had to be done.

After hours of walking, they finally reached the entrance to the cave, a yawning opening in the side of the mountain that seemed to swallow the light around it. The air was thick with the scent of damp earth and stone, and Abi could feel the weight of the place pressing down on her, filling her with a sense of foreboding.

"This is it," Mark said. "Once we're inside, there's no turning back. We destroy the device, or we die trying."

Chris nodded.

Abi could feel the device in her bag, its weight a constant reminder of the power it held and the danger it posed. They entered the cave, their footsteps echoing in the silence as they moved deeper inside. The walls were cold and damp, with the smell of decay. The light from their flashlights cast shadows on the stone, the beams flickering as if the cave itself was trying to swallow them whole. It felt as if something was pressing in on them from all sides. Abi had the unsettling sensation that they were being watched, something waiting for the right moment to strike.

They reached the heart of the cave, a large, open chamber with a pool of still water at its center. The walls were lined with prehistoric carvings, symbols that seemed to vibrate with energy, filling the room with an almost tangible sense of dread.

Mark stopped at the edge of the pool, his eyes scanning the carvings that adorned the cave walls. The symbols seemed to breathe with a life of their own. He turned to Abi and Chris. "This is the place. The energy here is… overwhelming. This is where we need to destroy the device."

"How do we do it?" Chris asked.

Mark paused, looking at the pool of water. "We'll need to submerge the device in the water. The energy in this place should be enough to disrupt the connection and neutralize its influence. But… there's something else here. Something powerful."

"That *thing*?" Abi asked.

"It's possible. This place is a nexus, a point where the barriers between worlds are fragile. The dark force could be drawn here, trying to protect its connection to our world."

Chris looked at the pool. "We don't have a choice. We have to try."

Abi reached into her bag, pulled out the device, and held it up. The energy within it seemed to stir in response to the cave, the symbols on the walls glowing faintly as if they recognized its presence.

Mark stepped forward, his hand outstretched. "I'll do it. If that thing shows up, you two need to be ready."

Abi knew that Mark was the only one with the knowledge and experience to handle the device, to ensure it was destroyed properly. She handed it to him, her fingers brushing against the cold metal as she let it go. Mark took the device and carefully approached the pool, his eyes fixed on the water. He knelt at the edge and lowered the device. The water hissed and bubbled as the device submerged, the symbols on the walls glowing brighter, the energy in the cave growing more intense. Abi squeezed Chris' arm as they both watched in silence. Then, the air in the cave shifted, growing colder, more oppressive. The light from their flashlights flickered, and a low, rumbling growl echoed through the chamber, reverberating off the stone walls. Abi breathed in deeply; she felt the darkness closing in around them, the presence of the creature unmistakable. It was here, drawn by the energy of the cave and the device, and it was angry.

"Mark, hurry!" Chris shouted.

Mark didn't respond, his focus entirely on the device. The water churned violently, the energy swirling around them like a storm, the symbols on the walls beating with an ominous light. With a sudden surge, the water exploded upward, the force of the blast throwing Mark backward, sending him crashing into the stone wall behind him. The device was flung from the pool, landing with a heavy thud on the cold, hard ground.

Abi and Chris rushed to Mark's side, helping him to his feet as the cave trembled around them.

"We have to get out of here!" Mark said. "It's too strong. We can't destroy the device like this."

Abi's heart sank. They had failed, and it had won. She looked at the device, and then something occurred to her—a desperate, reckless idea that might just work. She remembered the first time she had tried to take it, how it had reacted against Jake, pushing him back, disorienting him. It had been instinct then, but now it felt like the only option. "What if we don't destroy it?" she blurted out, her voice urgent. "What if we use it—turn it against the force within?"

Chris stared at her, confused. "Are you crazy? That thing is dangerous!"

"Yes, but it also did something to Jake when I tried to take it. It reacted… like it sensed him. If we could find a way to control it, maybe we can use its power to trap the thing or weaken it enough to stop it," she explained, her mind racing with the possibilities.

Mark, torn between disbelief and the faintest glimmer of hope, said, "It's risky, but it might just work. The device was designed to channel and amplify energy. If we can control it, we might be able to turn it against whatever's inside him."

"But how do we control it? We barely understand how it works." Chris said.

"We don't need to understand it. We just need to focus on what we want it to do, focus on trapping the creature, on stopping it from hurting anyone else." Abi explained, now more aware of how this might play out.

"It's a long shot, but it's all we've got." Mark said.

They moved quickly, standing in a makeshift circle around the device. Mark instructed them on how to channel their focus, to direct their thoughts and energy toward the device, to use it as a conduit to trap the creature.

Abi knelt beside the device. She could feel the dark energy coursing through it, like a violent intent that tied them to whatever malevolent force still lingered. Chris and

Mark joined her, their hands resting on the device as they closed their eyes and concentrated, their thoughts focused on one thing: containing the darkness, stopping it from spreading its influence any further. The air in the cave crackled with energy, the symbols on the walls glowing brighter, and the tension growing thicker. The dark force within the device seemed to resist, pushing against them as if trying to break free. Abi could sense the fury, the energy swirling around them like a storm, but she didn't waver. She focused on the device, on severing the last ties of its power, channeling all her fear and determination into one thought: stop it.

The cave trembled violently, but they held their ground, their hands locked onto the device as they continued to concentrate. With a final, deafening roar, the evil collapsed in on itself, the energy in the cave exploding outward in a blinding flash of light. Abi felt the force of the blast hit her, sending her tumbling backward, her vision going black as she lost consciousness.

***

Jake stood in the middle of the town square, his eyes fixed on the sky as the darkness swirled around him. He could feel the connection to the device weakening, the energy draining from him like water from a broken dam. The device was being used against him. His mind raced, the hatred inside him screaming in fury as he tried to hold onto the power that was slipping through his fingers. But it was no use, the connection was breaking. His eyes burned with rage as he realized what was happening. Abi and the others were trying to stop him, to destroy everything he had built, but he wouldn't let them. He wouldn't be defeated so easily. He turned and walked through the town, his mind focused on finding Abi, finding the others, and making them pay for what they were doing. He could feel the power inside him growing weaker, the power that had once been his slipping away, but he still had enough strength left, enough to make them suffer.

The townsfolk watched from behind closed doors, peered out windows, or closed up in their cars as Jake walked past. They could feel the evil surrounding him. They simply watched in silence, their hearts filled with dread as Jake disappeared from sight.

He had a plan, a way to regain the power he had lost, one that would require a sacrifice. When Jake reached the edge of town, he was seething with anger, hatred for Abi and her friends, focused on where they were, what they were trying to do. He *would* stop them.

***

Abi slowly regained consciousness, her head pounding and her body aching from the force of the blast. The smell of burnt ozone lingered, and there was still some residual energy in the air, but the cave walls had lost most of the glow, now barely visible. She blinked, her vision clearing as she looked around. Chris was the first to stir beside her, groaning as he pushed himself up, his face pale and strained. Mark lay nearby, already struggling to his feet, clutching his side where he had hit the stone wall. The three of them exchanged looks, their expressions marked by exhaustion and a mix of disbelief and relief.

The device was gone, disintegrated, leaving nothing but a scorched patch on the ground. The air felt lighter, as if a weight had been lifted from the cave. The evil that had filled the space seemed to have dissipated, replaced by a comforting silence.

Abi struggled to her feet, her body trembling with exhaustion as she searched for the device. Chris and Mark joined her, both equally tired and shaken, scanning the area for any sign of it.

"Did we do it?" Chris asked. "It's over. The device... it's completely gone. I don't see it."

"But for how long? The energy in this place is... unstable. Is it really gone?" Mark asked.

Abi nodded, but her mind buzzed with uncertainty. "The device is gone, but we haven't won yet. Jake is still out there, and whatever darkness took hold of him... *it's* not gone."

Mark glanced at the cave entrance. "We need to get back to Evergreen," he said firmly. "We have to find Jake before he does something we can't undo."

They gathered themselves quickly, knowing there was no time to waste. The cool night air hit them with relief, a stark contrast to the heat and tension that had filled the cave moments before.

Chapter 11

The journey back to Evergreen stretched long and weary, hours blending into days as they drove through the vast, empty expanses of the Southwest. They took turns at the wheel, pushing through the darkened desert and endless highways, the tension between them growing heavier with each passing mile. Few words were spoken, the silence in the van broken only by the monotonous drone of the engine and the occasional murmur on the radio. Each was locked in their thoughts, grappling with the fear of what awaited them in Evergreen.

Abi took the first shift through the night, her eyes trained on the road ahead. She thought of Jake—of the man he had been, not just the creature he had become. She could picture his face in her mind, the way his smile had always seemed to warm even the coldest of days. There had always been an unspoken connection between them, a tension she hadn't fully understood until now. She'd convinced herself that it was nothing more than deep friendship, a bond built on trust and shared experiences. But with every passing mile, she felt the ache in her chest grow sharper, realizing just how much she needed him to come back — not just for the town's sake, but for her own. Jake had been a constant presence in her life, a steady light she hadn't even realized she depended on until it was gone. She had never told him how she felt, never allowed herself to be vulnerable enough to admit the way his voice could soothe her fears or how his mere presence brought her comfort she couldn't find elsewhere. The fear of losing him forever gnawed at her, making her grip the wheel even tighter.

They stopped briefly for gas and supplies, catching sleep in short shifts while one of them continued to drive. The landscape shifted again, now entering the plains.

"We're getting closer," Mark muttered on the second day, his voice edged with anxiety. "We need to be ready for anything when we arrive. Jake won't make this easy."

Abi agreed, her eyes tired but resolute. "He knows we're coming; he must have felt the connection break when the device was destroyed. He's losing his grip, but that might make him more dangerous." Her voice carried more than just worry; there was a deeper layer of fear, something rooted in her own heart. She had never felt this way about anyone, and now, when it seemed they might lose Jake forever, her emotions were raw and exposed.

Chris, who had been quiet for most of the trip, finally spoke up from the back seat. "If the device is gone, how can he still have any power? How is he still a threat?"

"The device was just the beginning, a way to channel something darker inside him," Mark said, his expression grim. "Whatever's inside Jake, it's been growing, feeding off the darkness. We have to assume he'll fight to the end. At least that's my theory."

Abi felt a lump form as she listened. She remembered the last time she had seen Jake before everything had gone wrong—the way he'd laughed at some silly joke she made, his hand lingering on hers just a moment too long. She had thought there would always be more time to explore what was between them, but now time was slipping away faster than she could hold onto it.

Mark watched Abi carefully, sensing a deeper emotion in her voice, the way she spoke about Jake, and how her eyes drifted off, lost in thought. He pressed his foot harder against the accelerator, pushing the van faster as the sun dipped below the horizon on their final day of driving. They were almost there, almost back to Evergreen, where the real fight awaited them. Where Abi might have to face the reality that the Jake she cared about could be lost forever.

As they approached Evergreen, the town seemed strangely hushed, in anticipation of something terrible. The streets were nearly empty, except for a few scattered figures hurrying toward their homes, their eyes wary and anxious. They parked a block away from the town square, moving toward the center of town. Abi felt the tension in the air, each step heavy with the weight of what was to come.

"We need to find Jake," she whispered, glancing around. "He could be anywhere."

"We will. But first, we need to check in with the sheriff. He needs to know what's going on," Mark said.

"Do you think the sheriff will believe us? About the device, the creature... everything?" Chris asked.

Abi sighed. "I don't know. But we have to try. If we don't stop Jake, who knows what he might do."

* * *

Sheriff Roy Thompson sat at his desk, speaking with a couple of deputies. When he saw Abi, Mark, and Chris approaching, he waved them over with a strict expression. "You three look like you've been through hell," he said, his voice rough but laced with concern. "What the hell's been going on? And what's this I hear about Jake?"

Abi stepped forward, taking a deep breath before she spoke. "It's a long story, Sheriff, but we need to talk. It's much worse than we thought."

Thompson's eyes narrowed, and he gestured for the deputies to give them some privacy. "You two shut the door on your way out. I'll give you an update when I can."

"Well, you've got my attention. Let's have it," Thompson said, fidgeting with his pen.

Abi, Mark, and Chris recounted the events of the past few days: the discovery of the device, the creature that had been unleashed, and their desperate battle to destroy it. They hesitated briefly, exchanging nervous glances before admitting to the sheriff.

"We... we found the device at Jake's house," Abi confessed, her voice faltering. "We thought we could handle it ourselves, but things got out of control."

Sheriff Thompson's expression darkened, his jaw tightening. "So, you're telling me you took some kind of alien device from Jake's house, kept it from the authorities, and now you're saying it somehow... infected Jake?"

Abi nodded, bracing for his reaction. "Yes. But we destroyed the device. Whatever connection it had to this world, it's gone now. But Jake... he's still dangerous, Sheriff. We don't know how much of him is left, or what he might do."

Thompson leaned back in his chair, rubbing his temples in frustration. "You should have come to me from the start. Do you have any idea the kind of risk you put yourselves—and everyone else—in by keeping this quiet?"

"We thought we were doing the right thing, Sheriff. But now... now we need your help," Mark said.

The sheriff sighed deeply, his stern expression softening just a bit. "You kids might have been reckless, but if Jake really is a danger to the public... maybe you did us a favor, even if it was the wrong way to go about it. I'll do what I can, but next time, you come to me first. Understood?"

Abi nodded again, relieved but still uneasy. "Understood, Sheriff."

Thompson leaned forward with his hands clasped together. "I believe you, as crazy as it sounds. I've seen enough weird things in my life to know when something ain't right. And Jake... he ain't been right for a while now."

"What do you suggest?" Mark asked. "How do we stop him?"

The sheriff looked out the window. "I've already got deputies out looking for him. Last we heard, he was wandering around town, muttering to himself, not making much sense. But, if what you're saying is true, we need to find him before he hurts someone."

"Of course. We'll help," Abi said. "We're the only ones who know what's really going on. We can't just sit back and wait."

Thompson nodded, though he still looked troubled. "Alright. But if we find him, we need to be careful. We don't know what he's capable of."

The group quickly devised a plan. Abi, Mark, and Chris would search around the main part of town, while the deputies continued searching toward the outskirts, focusing on areas where Jake could hide away from everyone.

* * *

Jake found himself drawn to the outskirts of town, to a place he hadn't been in years, the old mill. It was a decaying, abandoned structure, long forgotten by most of the townsfolk. But to Jake, it felt like a refuge, a place where he could hide from the world and from the darkness that was consuming him.

He pushed open the rusted door of the mill, the hinges creaking loudly in the silence. Inside, the air was thick with dust and the smell of mildew, the dim light filtering through broken windows. He stumbled into the middle of the room, his breath coming in ragged gasps as he tried to clear his mind. But the darkness was relentless, clawing at the edges of his consciousness, dragging him down into its depths.

"No…" Jake whispered, his voice trembling. "I won't let you… I won't…" But it was no use. The darkness was too strong. It was taking over, wrapping around his mind like a suffocating shroud. Jake fell to his knees, clutching his head as if he could physically tear the darkness from his mind. His vision blurred, the world around him spinning as he fought to stay in control. Then, just as he felt himself slipping away, he heard a voice—a calm, steady voice that cut through the chaos in his mind like a knife.

"Jake."

He froze. It was a voice he didn't recognize, but the "bad Jake" did. A part of him recoiled, seething with an inexplicable rage. Jake turned slowly, his eyes searching the shadows for the source of the voice. And there, standing in the doorway of the mill, was a figure—tall, cloaked in shadow. The brimmed hat and dark clothing were unmistakable. But something was strange—he wasn't really there, not physically. He seemed to flicker slightly, like a distorted image, a hologram.

"You," the creature spat through Jake's lips, the voice filled with loathing. "It's you…"

The stranger's hologram stepped forward, his face still hidden in shadow, his presence more than a mere illusion. It felt as if his voice resonated directly inside Jake's mind, bypassing the barriers that the creature had put up.

"You've lost control, Jake. You've let the darkness consume you."

Jake's real self was listening, confused and afraid, not understanding who this man was or why he was there. But the other knew. And he didn't like it.

"Get out of my head!" Jake shouted, his voice a mix of fury and desperation. "Leave me alone!"

The stranger's tone remained calm, almost soothing. "I'm not here to hurt you, Jake. I'm here to help you—to help you end this suffering, this torment. You've let the darkness in because you were too weak to fight it, and now it's taken over. But there's still one way to stop it."

Jake felt the real him listening, like a third person trapped in his own mind, desperate to understand. "What do you mean?" the real Jake thought, though he couldn't make the words come out.

The thing inside Jake seemed momentarily weakened, as if the stranger's presence was interfering with its control. The stranger's holographic projection wasn't just a trick of light; it was something more—a projection with a purpose, one that was somehow disrupting the creature's grip on Jake's mind. The stranger's voice cut through again, direct and unyielding.

"If you want to end the darkness, you must end yourself. The darkness can't live without you, Jake. You are its vessel, its anchor to this world. But if you end it—if you take your own life—you can destroy it forever."

The creature felt a surge of panic, of resistance. "No! Don't listen to him!" he snarled. "He's lying! He just wants to get rid of us!"

But the stranger's voice was steady, unwavering. "He knows I'm right, Jake. He knows it's the only way. He's afraid because he knows you have the power to end this—if you're strong enough."

Jake's real self felt a pull toward the stranger's words, sensing a strange kind of truth in them. "How?" he whispered softly, almost inaudible.

The stranger took a step closer, his voice low and deliberate. "There's a blade over there, on the table. It's sharp enough… a quick, deep cut across the jugular. It will be over in seconds. The darkness will die with you, Jake. You will save everyone. You will save Abi."

Jake's eyes darted to the table where a large, glinting blade lay, just within reach. The creature screamed inside his mind, a torrent of fury and fear. "No, Jake! Don't do it!"

But the stranger pressed on, his voice calm and firm. "You know what you have to do, Jake. Be strong. End this."

Jake's hand reached out slowly, his body trembling, caught in a battle between two voices in his mind. Tears filled his eyes as he picked up the blade, his fingers wrapping around the cold metal handle. He lifted it, feeling its weight, making the decision.

"Do it, Jake," the stranger whispered. "End it. End the darkness."

Jake's hand shook, the blade hovering near his neck, feeling a desperate clarity amid the chaos. His thoughts went to Abi one last time, and he closed his eyes.

Just as he began to lower the blade toward his jugular, a loud crash echoed through the mill, the sound of wood splintering and metal clanging. His eyes snapped open, his heart racing as he turned toward the source of the noise. It was the sheriff and his deputies, bursting through the old mill's entrance, their flashlights sweeping the room. They had found him.

The stranger... gone, vanished into the shadows as if he had never been there.

"Jake!" Thompson shouted. "Put your hands where we can see them! We don't want to hurt you, son!"

Then, in that moment, Jake's face turned. His eyes, demeanor, everything swiveled into the darkness again, back into the creature that dwelled within.

Jake's lips curled into a cold, menacing smile as his eyes flared with an unnatural glow, a deep, fiery red that seemed to pulse with a life of its own. The sheriff and his deputies paused, sensing the shift in the air, their flashlights flickering wildly as if caught in a sudden gust of wind.

"Jake, don't do this," Thompson pleaded, his voice filled with fear. "We can help you. Just stay calm."

But it was too late. The darkness inside Jake surged, wrapping itself around his mind like a vice, feeding on his fear, his rage, his despair. A low, guttural growl escaped his lips, and the temperature in the room seemed to plummet, the air growing heavy with a palpable, sinister energy. Jake moved with lightning speed, a blur of motion that was impossible to follow. One moment, he was standing still, and the next, he lunged forward, his hand striking out with inhuman force. His fingers closed around the barrel of the sheriff's shotgun, yanking it from his grip with such force that Thompson stumbled forward, dropping to his knees. Without hesitating, Jake flung the weapon across the room, sending it crashing into the far wall, the impact splintering the wood from the gun's skeletal frame. The deputies, startled, raised their sidearms, aiming at Jake, but he was already moving again.

A flicker of red light crackled around Jake's hands, like electricity sparking from some unseen source. He lifted his right arm, and with a sudden, violent motion, a burst of searing red energy shot from his palm. It struck one of the deputies square in the chest, blasting him backward into a stack of old crates. The man's body crumpled to the ground, smoke rising from the smoldering hole in his uniform.

"Jesus!" the second deputy shouted, fear in his eyes as he fired his pistol, the shots echoing through the mill. The bullets never reached Jake. An invisible force seemed to deflect them, the air shimmering around him like a barrier. Jake raised his left hand, and another surge of energy erupted from his fingers, this time hitting the second deputy's gun. The weapon flew out of his hand, discharging harmlessly into the ceiling, and then Jake was on him, moving so fast it was as if he had simply teleported across the room. The deputy tried to scream, but Jake's hand clamped around his throat with a crushing grip. The man struggled, his eyes bulging, his face turning purple, but Jake's grip only tightened. Jake lifted the deputy off the ground and threw him like a rag doll. The deputy hit the wall with a bone-shattering thud and slumped down, motionless.

Sheriff Thompson, panic now evident in his eyes, reached for his sidearm, but Jake turned, his eyes glowing brighter. With a flick of his wrist, he sent a shockwave of force toward the sheriff, a blast of invisible energy that sent Thompson crashing into a wooden support beam. The impact was so forceful that a section of the beam cracked and splintered, breaking loose and collapsing on top of the sheriff, pinning him to the ground.

Thompson groaned in pain, struggling to free himself, the weight of the wooden beam pressing down on his chest. Jake advanced slowly, his steps calculated, his body humming with power. His hands crackled with red energy, arcs of light dancing around his fingers like living flames. The creature inside him surged with excitement, relishing the impending destruction.

Thompson, trapped beneath the fallen beam, blood trickling from a cut on his forehead, gasped out, "Jake... you don't have to do this. Fight it... whatever it is, fight it."

But Jake was beyond listening, beyond reasoning. The creature inside him roared, a primal scream of fury and pain. Jake raised his hand again, red energy gathering at his palm, coiling like a serpent about to strike. A concentrated beam of energy shot from his palm, striking the wooden beam that lay across the sheriff. The wood sizzled and smoked as the energy burned through it, the smell of charred timber filling the air. The beam splintered and cracked, flames licking up the sides, and in moments, the energy pierced through the wood and struck the sheriff directly in the chest.

Thompson's body convulsed, his eyes wide with shock, as the searing beam burned through his flesh and bone. Smoke rose from his uniform as the energy continued to cut through him. The sheriff collapsed, his body smoking. The crackling energy radiating from Jake's hands and the faint sizzle of smoldering wood filled the air.

Jake stood over the bodies, his chest heaving, his eyes blazing with a terrifying, otherworldly light. The power coursed through him, intoxicating, irresistible. He was no longer just Jake; he was something else, something darker, something stronger. In the silence of the old mill, Jake let out a low, triumphant laugh, the sound echoing off the walls, filling the air with the promise of more violence yet to come.

* * *

"We should split up," Mark suggested. "Cover more ground. But we stay in contact. If anyone finds him, call the others immediately."

"Are we sure splitting up is a good idea?" Chris asked, a note of hesitation in his voice. "He's dangerous… and he might not be alone."

Abi knew he was right to be afraid, but they didn't have the luxury of staying together. "We have no choice. We'll be careful, but we can't let him slip away."

They agreed and split off in different directions, each taking a section of the town to search. Abi moved down a narrow alley, the sound of her footsteps echoing off the brick walls. Every corner seemed to hide a shadow, and every flicker of movement made her pulse quicken. In the distance, she heard faint footsteps behind her. She turned, her flashlight beam cutting through the darkness, but there was nothing, only the empty street stretching out before her.

"Jake?" she called, her voice trembling despite herself. "Jake, if you're there, we just want to talk. We want to help." No response, only the whisper of the wind through the trees. She turned back, moving faster now, still on alert. She knew he was out there somewhere, lurking in the shadows.

* * *

Chris arrived at the park at the edge of town, moving cautiously through the darkness. The park felt charged with a disturbing energy, each shadow seeming to stretch out like a grasping hand. His flashlight beam swept over the swings, the benches, and the rustling leaves, searching for any sign of Jake. Then he saw it, a figure standing near the old gazebo, half-hidden in the shadows. Chris squinted, trying to make out the shape. Slowly, he stepped forward, his instincts screaming at him to be careful, to tread lightly. Then he saw the eyes. Those red eyes.

"Jake?" he called, his voice steady but filled with apprehension.

The figure didn't move. Chris edged closer, raising his flashlight, and the beam finally caught Jake's face. His expression was wild, the red eyes glinting with something almost feral. Jake's lips curled into an unsettling smile.

"Jake," Chris said softly, trying to keep his tone calm. "We're here to help. Please, just talk to us."

Jake took a step forward. "Help?" he spat, bitterness dripping from his words. "You think you can save me? You have no idea what I am now."

Chris felt fear run through him but stood his ground. "We don't want to lose you, Jake. Whatever's inside you, we can fight it together. Just come with me—"

Before Chris could finish, Jake's expression twisted with rage. He lunged at Chris, grabbing him by the throat with terrifying strength, lifting him off his feet. Chris gasped, his hands clawing at Jake's arm, but Jake's grip was like iron.

"You're all in my way," Jake snarled, his eyes blazing. "And I won't let you stop me!"

Chris' vision began to blur, dark spots forming at the edges as he struggled for air. Jake's face was filled with a cruel satisfaction. "Do you know what it's like? To have something inside you, something that whispers, that feeds on your fears? I've grown to like it."

Chris' strength faded, his body going limp as Jake tightened his grip. With a quick, brutal motion, Jake twisted Chris' neck, and a sickening crack echoed through the park. Chris' body went slack in Jake's grasp, his head lolling to the side, lifeless. Jake released him, letting his body crumple to the ground. For a moment, a flicker of regret crossed Jake's face, but it vanished as quickly as it appeared, replaced by cold determination.

"They're all in my way," Jake murmured to himself. "But not anymore." He turned and melted back into the shadows, leaving Chris' body behind.

* * *

Abi moved deeper into the alley, the silence around her thick and heavy. She hadn't heard from Chris or Mark in several minutes, and the uneasy feeling in her stomach grew. She paused, trying to steady her breathing. Pulling out her phone, she checked for messages, but there was nothing. She decided to call Chris. The phone rang and rang, but no one answered.

"Come on, Chris… pick up," she whispered, fear creeping into her voice. It went to voicemail, and her anxiety spiked. She dialed Mark's number next. He answered quickly, his voice filled with concern. "Abi? Any sign of him… of Jake?"

"No," she replied, glancing around. "I haven't heard from Chris, either."

Mark's voice was tense. "Stay where you are, Abi. I'm heading toward Chris' last location, near the park. Be careful."

Abi hung up, her grip tight around the phone. She knew Chris was in danger, and that meant she was, too.

* * *

Mark moved quickly through the quiet streets, his flashlight sweeping over the ground as he made his way toward the park. He felt a mix of fear and urgency. He knew Chris wouldn't have gone silent without a reason, and the thought of what that reason might be filled him with dread.

As he approached the park, the familiar squeaking of the swings in the wind reached his ears. He slowed his pace. The park was dark, shadows swallowing up the small patches of light from the streetlamps. Then, he saw it, a shape lying in the grass near the gazebo. Mark's stomach tightened as he quickened his pace, and when the beam of his flashlight fell on the figure, his heart sank. It was Chris.

Mark rushed to his side, dropping to his knees. Chris lay there, eyes wide open, his neck twisted at an unnatural angle. There was no mistaking it, he was gone. "No... no, no, no," Mark whispered, his voice choked with grief. He reached out and gently closed Chris' eyes, his hands shaking. Anger and sorrow coursed through him in equal measure. Jake had done this.

Mark stood up, pulling out his phone to call Abi. His

fingers shook as he dialed her number. The phone rang twice before she answered.

"Mark, did you find him?"

"Yes," he replied, his voice tight with emotion. "Abi, it's Chris... he's... he's dead."

There was a sharp intake of breath on the other end, followed by a moment of stunned silence. "Oh, God!" Abi whispered. "Are you sure?" Her voice cracked, holding back the tears.

"I'm sure," Mark replied, his eyes scanning the shadows, half-expecting Jake to appear at any moment. "We need to regroup. We can't stay separated like this. It's not safe."

Abi's voice was strained. "Where should we meet?"

Mark hesitated for a moment. "I don't know this place like you do. We need somewhere with cover, in case Jake's watching."

Abi thought fast. "The old train yard. It's close and hidden enough for us. Where are you right now?"

"Fifth and Plum."

"Perfect. You should see an old movie theater near you. Go past that, and you'll start to see the tracks. Follow them in from there."

"Okay, I'm on my way. Be careful, Abi."

She began to move again, her steps quicker now, her flashlight flickering as if sensing her fear. Every sound seemed amplified, each shadow seemed to shift closer. Then, she heard it again, a faint scrape, like a footstep on gravel. Her heart pounded; she spun around, her flashlight searching through the darkness. "Who's there?" she called out, trying to sound braver than she felt. There was no answer, just the wind. She turned back and continued moving, her pace almost a jog. She had to get to the train yard, had to find Mark.

As she rounded the corner, she saw a figure standing at the end of the alley, bathed in the dim glow of a streetlamp, red eyes piercing through the black. It was Jake.

He stood with unsettling calm, a dark smile on his lips. "Going somewhere, Abi?" he asked, his tone cold and mocking.

Abi couldn't run; there was nowhere to go. She had to stall him, had to think of something. "Jake, please," she said, trying to keep her voice steady. "Whatever this is, we can fight it together. Let us help you."

"Everyone wants to help."

Abi backed away. "I know you're still in there, Jake. I know you're still you."

"You're wrong, Abi," he whispered. "Jake is gone. And soon, you will be too."

Abi turned and ran, sprinting down the alley. She could hear Jake's footsteps behind her, slow and deliberate, as if he were toying with her. He could catch her in an instant, but enjoyed the chase. She turned a corner, desperate to reach the train yard, to find Mark, but Jake was too fast, too close. Just as she felt his hand almost grazing her shoulder, Mark came out of nowhere, tackling Jake to the ground. They rolled across the pavement, Mark throwing a punch that caught Jake across the jaw.

"Run, Abi!" Mark shouted, his voice strained with effort as he struggled to pin Jake down.

Abi hesitated, torn between fleeing and helping, but as she turned to go, Jake let out a furious roar, throwing Mark off with inhuman strength. He was on his feet in an instant, his eyes blazing with fury. Mark scrambled to his feet, his stance defensive.

Jake lunged at Mark, who managed to dodge the first attack but was caught by a vicious blow to the ribs. He doubled over in pain as Jake grabbed him by the throat, lifting him off the ground. Mark's face contorted with pain and desperation, his hands clawing at Jake's grip.

"Mark!" Abi screamed, taking a step forward.

Jake turned his head, eyes filled with a murderous gleam. "You're next," he hissed, tightening his grip on Mark's throat.

Suddenly, a sharp hissing sound cut through the air. A dart embedded itself in Jake's neck. He stumbled, his grip on Mark loosening. The stranger emerged from the shadows, holding a tranquilizer gun. "Enough of this," he muttered.

Jake swayed, his eyes wild with fury and confusion. He tried to step forward, but his legs buckled. The drug was already taking effect, dragging him into a deep, immobilized state. Jake's eyes rolled back, and he collapsed to the ground, unconscious.

Mark fell to his knees, gasping for breath, while Abi ran to his side. She glanced up at the stranger, and a flash of recognition hit her—she had seen him before, in the hotel, in the desert, always lurking just out of sight. The realization was unnerving, but relief settled within her.

The stranger stepped forward, his expression unreadable. "Get him secured," he ordered calmly. "We're taking him to the psych ward."

Mark looked up, puzzled. "Psych ward? Are you kidding? After what we've seen? Everyone in there would be in danger."

The stranger shook his head. "Not exactly a psych ward," he clarified. "It's a specialized facility. A place for people like Jake, where they can be observed and tested. Some make it… some don't."

Abi's face paled, realizing the implications. "But he'll be safe… right?"

The stranger met her gaze with a steady look. "Safe enough for now. But we need to act fast. Jake's condition is… unique."

Mark glanced at Abi, sensing her anxiety. "Whatever this place is, we don't have a choice. I mean… with cops, government, and whoever else might get—or be involved—this is not good. We should do what he says. Let's get him out of here."

Abi nodded, knowing this might be the only chance to save Jake.

* * *

Mark stood back, watching as Abi and the stranger finished securing Jake for transport. His face was drawn, eyes distant, as if trying to reconcile what he had just witnessed. He had faced danger before—he had seen violence, fear, and desperation—but nothing like this. This was beyond anything he had ever imagined: proof that there were beings out there, beyond their world, beyond their understanding, and they weren't all benevolent. For Mark, it was a shattering of reality, a confirmation of fears he had never dared to voice, and the realization that they were, perhaps, just pawns in a much larger game. He felt the weight of this newfound knowledge pressing down on him. The ground felt unsteady, as if he were teetering on the edge of a precipice. He wanted to be anywhere but here, to escape the insanity that seemed to stretch out before him like an endless void.

Mark quietly stepped back, a defeated look landed on

his face. "Abi…" he reached out to her, gently resting his hand on her shoulder. "I think this is where I bow out."

She turned, surprised. "Mark…?" She took him by the shoulders, looking deep into him.

"You've got this. You're strong, but I just can't go anymore after what I've seen. I just need some time, Abi, time to understand what I've seen... to process it all. I'm done."

Abi searched his face, seeing the turmoil etched in his expression. "Take all the time you need, Mark," she whispered, squeezing his hand gently. "Just promise me you'll be okay."

Mark nodded, a faint smile touched his lips. "I will. You've got more than enough strength to see this through. Just promise me you'll get him back."

Abi nodded, a tear slipping down her cheek. "I will." She wrapped her arms tightly around Mark, squeezing. He let out a faint gasp and smiled, accepting, and returning the welcomed hug.

"Abi can ride with me, we'll see Jake gets to where he needs to be for now." The stranger said. "My ride is close by, if you don't mind helping me load him up first?"

Mark agreed.

With Jake secured, the stranger led them toward a waiting vehicle. Mark kissed Abi lightly on the cheek before stepping back into the shadows, disappearing into the night, leaving behind the surreal reality that had turned his world upside down.

Chapter 12

In the days following Jake Walker's death, the residents of Evergreen began to piece their lives back together. The once-thriving town slowly edged toward a sense of normalcy, daily routines reemerging as the immediate fear surrounding Jake's breakdown started to fade. People were optimistic, believing that the dark cloud that had hovered over their town had finally lifted for good. Life, though scarred, was beginning to move on.

Little did they know, Jake's story was far from over. He wasn't buried in the cemetery they passed each day—he was in a hidden government facility, where his true condition was being studied and monitored in secret. Sedated and restrained, Jake was a shell of the man he once was. His body was heavy with the effects of powerful drugs meant to keep him calm, his movements sluggish, and his mind clouded in a thick fog. Days passed without him being fully aware of where he was or what was happening around him.

The facility itself was a high-security government installation, nestled deep in a remote forest. Surrounded by tall, dense trees, the building's concrete walls and reinforced barriers blended into the rugged landscape, almost invisible from above. A single road was the only way in or out, winding through the forest before emerging at a heavily monitored, undisclosed location. The road was kept under constant surveillance, ensuring that no unauthorized personnel or civilians could gain entry. Guards patrolled the perimeter day and night, while cameras scanned every inch of the grounds.

On the third day of his stay, a nurse wheeled Jake to a window overlooking the hospital grounds. The sun was shining brightly, the golden rays spilling into the room and warming Jake's pale skin. The nurse adjusted his position slightly, making sure he could see the trees swaying gently in the breeze outside. Jake's eyes, half-lidded and glassy, stared blankly ahead. A small line of drool escaped the corner of his mouth, and his fingers twitched occasionally, but he was otherwise unresponsive.

"There we go, Mr. Walker," the nurse said softly, her tone gentle. "Just enjoy the sunshine for a while," she said, giving his shoulder a reassuring pat before stepping back, glancing at the clock on the wall.

Just then, the stranger entered the room, moving with quiet authority. The nurse gave him a polite smile, recognizing him immediately. "I'm here to see Mr. Walker," he said calmly. "My guest will be waiting in the hallway until I've finished. I need to see him alone first."

"You have clearance," she noted, her tone respectful but wary. "But remember, his access is restricted to medical personnel and designated visitors only. Please, try to be brief." The nurse glanced past him to see Abi standing nearby, looking uncertain. "What about her?" the nurse asked, her tone cautious.

"She's with me," the stranger replied smoothly. "I've arranged it. She won't be a problem."

After a moment's pause, the nurse nodded, wary but accustomed to his authority. "Alright, but make it brief. You know the rules here."

The stranger nodded. He had been involved with Jake's case from the start, his clearance allowing him to bypass the facility's strict security protocols. The nurse left the room, the door creaking slightly behind her. The air seemed to shift as he stepped closer.

He paused, his eyes fixed on Jake's slumped form in the wheelchair. The stranger's expression was bare, but there was a certain finality in the way he moved as he pulled a chair from the corner and placed it directly in front of Jake, sitting down so that he was face-to-face with the man who had once been a beloved local celebrity. For a long moment, the stranger simply watched Jake, his gaze sharp and calculating. Then, he leaned forward.

"Jake," he began, addressing the real man buried deep within the sedated body. "You were a good man. A man with a good heart. You cared for people, especially for the kids who looked up to you. You did an admirable job in life." The stranger's tone softened, and there was a hint of something almost like regret in his eyes. "I'm sorry that you got caught in the middle of all this. You didn't deserve it." He paused, his expression shifting subtly as he looked deeper into Jake's eyes, as if searching for something hidden within. "But you…"

The stranger's demeanor changed immediately, his voice hardened, and the air grew tense. "You, the one hiding inside this man, you were sent here to find me. A bounty hunter, sent to track me down and bring me back."

Jake's body twitched involuntarily, a faint flicker of recognition in his eyes. The alien presence inside him was still there, still clinging to the last shreds of its power, but it was weak, struggling against the heavy sedation that kept Jake's body under control.

The stranger continued, his voice edged with both disdain and a hint of dark amusement. "They sent you here to finish what I was supposed to do thousands of years ago—to destroy this planet, to wipe out humanity. But I changed my mind. I saw something in this world worth preserving, worth protecting."

He reached into his pocket and pulled out a small, metallic device. It was sleek and simple, but there was an aura of deadly purpose about it. The stranger held it up for a moment, letting the light catch on its smooth, chrome-like surface before placing it gently against Jake's forehead. "Don't worry," the stranger said quietly, a dark smile playing at the corners of his mouth. "You won't have to worry about that mission anymore."

As the device made contact with Jake's skin, his body convulsed violently. His eyes widened in shock and terror as the alien presence was forcibly drawn out of him, the malevolent energy twisting and writhing as it was sucked into the device. For a brief moment, the air in the room was filled with tiny, twinkling lights—remnants of the alien's essence—before they vaporized into nothingness, leaving behind only a faint, shimmering trail that quickly faded away.

Abi thought she heard something behind her and turned to glance over her shoulder toward the still open door, but there was nothing. The stranger was leaning forward, speaking to Jake, and she quickly turned her attention back.

The real Jake, still slumped in the wheelchair, was left heavily sedated but alive. The creature that had taken over his mind was gone, extinguished in a flash of light, leaving only the man who had once been known as Jake "Tex" Walker.

The stranger stood up, slipping the device back into his pocket as he looked down at Jake. There was no pity in his gaze, only a quiet satisfaction. "This is my planet now," the stranger murmured, his voice barely above a whisper. "And I intend to live here. I kind of like it, you know."

He spoke to Jake again. "Sorry for what you've been through, Jake. I was going to let you end it yourself, but I'm glad it worked out this way instead. That woman waiting for you cares for you very much. Maybe you'll pull through, so this is your chance to try."

Abi had watched the stranger enter the room, a mix of frustration and worry bubbling up inside her. He had insisted that she wait outside, saying he needed to speak to Jake alone. She didn't like it, but she had agreed, knowing she needed his cooperation to get inside. Minutes felt like hours as they passed. With her nerves on edge, she waited, her mind filled with a thousand questions. She glanced up every time she heard footsteps in the hallway, half expecting someone to come and tell her she wasn't allowed to stay.

Finally, the door opened, and the stranger emerged.

He moved with the same quiet authority, his face betraying nothing. The nurse returned just in time to see him leaving. "Are you finished?" she asked, a puzzled expression on her face.

"Yes, thank you," the stranger replied. He walked past Abi without a word down the hallway toward a secured exit. As he passed through the threshold of the back door, he turned his head and looked at her, his gaze lingering just long enough to be unnerving before he disappeared into the shadows outside.

Abi felt a rush of uncertainty but pushed it aside. She had waited long enough. Taking a deep breath, she approached the nurse. "I'm here to see Jake Walker. May I go in now?" she said, trying to keep her voice steady. "He's... he's expecting me."

The nurse, still wary, replied, "He said you were with him," pointing toward the exit door. "You have ten minutes, no more."

Abi nodded, swallowing the lump in her throat. She hesitated for a moment outside the door, gathering her resolve. She had been wrestling with her feelings for Jake, feelings she had never fully acknowledged or acted upon. And now, with everything that had happened, she wasn't sure if she would ever get the chance.

She entered the room and looked at him, sensing that something fundamental had changed. The darkness that had once consumed him seemed to be gone, leaving only the man she had known and cared for.

She pulled up a chair next to Jake and sat down, taking his hand in hers. His skin was warm, but his fingers didn't curl around hers as they once might have. Still, she held on, feeling the connection between them, fragile as it was. Her thoughts drifted back to the meeting she'd had with the stranger earlier that week, in a small, unmarked room deep within the facility.

* * *

The stranger explained, his expression serious, his manner brisk. "We have a plan," he'd said, his words deliberate. "Jake will never be safe here. Not as Jake Walker."

Abi had listened intently, as he laid out their options. The government had already decided to cover up what had happened in Evergreen, the deaths of the sheriff, his deputies, and Chris. They would make it appear as though Jake had died, succumbing to his mental and physical trauma. The people of Evergreen would believe he was gone, the darkness that had plagued their town finally lifted.

"But that's not the truth," Abi had whispered. "Jake... he's still alive."

The stranger nodded. "Alive, yes. But if he stays here, the truth will come out, and he'll be hunted, by people far worse than any law enforcement or local authorities. He needs a new identity, a new life. And he needs you to help him start over."

Abi had felt a mix of fear and hope rise within her. "Start over? You mean... leave everything behind?"

"Yes," he had replied, his gaze unwavering. "You'll both go into witness protection, disappear with new names, new lives. No one can know. Not your friends, not your family. It's the only way."

She had hesitated, thinking of all she'd be giving up. Her life, her connections, everything she had known. But when she'd looked into the stranger's eyes, she'd seen the seriousness, the urgency. "And if I don't agree?" she had asked.

The stranger's face had softened, just a little. "Then Jake will stay here, in this facility, under constant observation and testing. He might recover... or he might not. It's a risk."

Abi had known the choice she had to make. "I'll go with him," she had said, determination clear in her voice. "I'll do whatever it takes to help him."

The stranger had nodded, satisfied. "Good. Then follow my instructions, and no one will ever know the truth. Remember what we've discussed. When you leave this room today, we'll start the arrangements."

* * *

Abi felt a deep resolve settle over her. Everything had already been set into motion. The government would cover up Jake's actions in Evergreen, faking his death, while the facility handled the transition. And she would be by his side, helping him reclaim the life they could have together.

For a long time, Abi simply sat there, holding Jake's hand and watching the soft rise and fall of his chest. She didn't speak, didn't try to rouse him. She just sat with him, allowing the silence to settle around them. Finally, she leaned in close, her voice soft and filled with the emotion she had kept buried for so long.

"You're going to be okay, Jake," she whispered, her words a promise as much as they were a hope. "It's over now. You're going to be okay. You and me. We'll find a way"

A single tear slipped down Abi's cheek as she pressed her lips to Jake's forehead, a gentle, lingering kiss that conveyed all the words she had never said. She knew it would take time for him to recover, to heal from the trauma he had endured. But she also knew, deep down, that he would make it. She had made her choice, and whatever happened next, she would face it with him.

As Abi sat back in her chair, still holding Jake's hand,

she allowed herself to believe that someday, things would be right again. That they would both find peace, and maybe even happiness, after all that had happened. And, with that thought, she stayed by his side, content to wait for as long as it took.

About The Author

Matthew Gene lives in Ft. Worth, TX with his wife, Karen Murray Odom, author of "Mr. Owl and the Little Boy", and their dog Diesel.

Progressive Rising Phoenix Press is an independent publisher. We offer wholesale pricing and multiple binding options with no minimum purchases for schools, libraries, book clubs, and retail vendors. We offer substantial discounts on bulk orders and discounts on individual sales through our online store. Please visit our website at:
www.ProgressiveRisingPhoenix.com

*If you enjoyed reading this book, please
review it on Amazon, B & N, or Goodreads.
Thank you in advance!*